In a Cellar
and other Stories

By

Harriet Prescott Spofford

British Library Cataloguing-in-Publication Data
A catalogue record for this book is available from the
British Library

Harriet Elizabeth Prescott Spofford

Harriet Elizabeth Prescott Spofford was born on 3rd April 1835 in Calais, Maine, United States. She is now best known for her novels, poems and detective stories – a true pioneer of the American detective genre. When she was still a baby, Spofford's parents moved to Newburyport, Massachusetts, where she chose to stay for almost her entire life. Although she spent many of her winters in Boston and Washington D.C., Newburyport remained always close to Spofford's heart.

She attended the Putnam Free School in Newburyport and Pinkerton Academy in Derry, New Hampshire from 1853 to 1855. At Newburyport her prize essay on Hamlet drew the attention of Thomas Wentworth Higginson (a Unitarian minister, author, abolitionist, and soldier), who soon became her friend and gave Spofford much needed counsel and encouragement throughout her career. When Spofford was in her mid-twenties, her parents suffered from ill health, and of necessity she was set to work as a writer, sometimes labouring fifteen hours a day. She contributed to various Boston story papers for small fees, but her first major success came in 1859; this was Spofford's submission to *Atlantic Monthly* (a literary and cultural magazine) of a story about Parisian life, 'In a Cellar'. The magazine's editor, James Russell Lowell, first believed the story to be a translation and withheld it from publication. Reassured it was original, he eventually published it, and the narrative established her reputation. After this success, Spofford became a welcome contributor to the chief periodicals of the United States, both of prose and poetry.

Spofford's fiction had very little in common with what was regarded as representative of 'the New England mind.' Her **gothic romances** were set apart by luxuriant descriptions and an unconventional handling of female **stereotypes** of the day. Her writing was ideal and intense in feeling, revelling in sensuous delights and material splendour. Nowhere was this more evident than, in 'Circumstance', an allegorical short story which takes place in the woods of Maine. In this tale, the protagonist comes into contact with the Indian Devil, forcing her to come to terms with her own life, sexuality and fears. When Wentworth Higginson asked Emily Dickinson whether she had read Spofford's work, Dickinson replied, 'I read Miss Prescott's '**Circumstance**,' but it followed me in the dark, so I avoided her.' Other notable works include *The Thief in the Night* (1872), *The Servant Girl Question* (1881), *A Scarlet Poppy and Other Stories* (1894), and *The Fairy Changeling* (1910).

In 1865, at the age of thirty, the authoress married Richard S. Spofford, a Boston lawyer, and the couple resided on Deer Island overlooking the **Merrimack River** at **Amesbury**, a suburb of Newburyport. They lived here for the rest of their lives. Harriet Prescott Spofford died on 14th August 1921, aged eighty-six.

TABLE OF CONTENTS

IN A CELLAR

IT WAS THE DAY of Madame de St. Cyr's dinner, an event I never missed; for, the mistress of a mansion in the Faubourg St. Germain, there still lingered about her the exquisite grace and good-breeding peculiar to the old regime, that insensibly communicates itself to the guests till they move in an atmosphere of ease that constitutes the charm of home. One was always sure of meeting desirable and well-assorted people here, and a contretemps was impossible. Moreover, the house was not at the command of all; and Madame de St. Cyr, with the daring strength which, when found in a woman at all, should, to be endurable, be combined with a sweet but firm restraint, rode rough-shod over the parvenus of the Empire, and was resolute enough to insulate herself even among the old noblesse, who, as all the world knows, insulate themselves from the rest of France. There were rare qualities in this woman, and were I to have selected one who with an even hand should carry a snuffy candle through a magazine of powder, my choice would have devolved upon her; and she would have done it.

I often looked, and not unsuccessfully, to discern what heritage her daughter had in these little affairs. Indeed, to one like myself, Delphine presented the worthier study. She wanted the airy charm of manner, the suavity and tenderness of her mother, — a deficiency easily to be pardoned in one of such delicate and extraordinary beauty. And perhaps her face was the truest index of her mind; not that it ever transparently displayed a genuine emotion, — Delphine was too well bred for that, — but the outline of her features had a keen regular precision, as if cut in a gem. Her exquisite color seldom varied, her eyes were like blue steel, she was statuelike and stony. But had one paused there, pronouncing her hard and impassive, he had committed an error. She had no great capability for passion, but she was not to be deceived; one metallic flash of her eye would cut like a sword through the whole mesh of entanglements with which you had surrounded her; and frequently, when alone with her, you perceived cool recesses in her nature, sparkling and pleasant, which jealously guarded themselves from a nearer approach. She was infinitely spirituelle; compared to her, Madame herself was heavy.

At the first, I had seen that Delphine must be the wife of a diplomate. What diplomate? For a time asking myself the question seriously, I decided in the negative, which did not, however, prevent Delphine from fulfilling her destiny, since there were others. She was, after all, like a draught of rich old wine, all fire and sweetness. These things were not generally seen in her; I was more favored than many; and I looked at her with pitiless perspicacious eyes. Nevertheless, I had not the least advantage; it was, in fact, between us, diamond cut diamond, — which, oddly enough, brings me back to my story.

Some years previously, I had been sent on a special mission to the government at Paris, and having finally executed it, I resigned the post, and resolved to make my residence there, since it is the only place on earth where one can live. Every morning I half expect to see the country, beyond the city, white with an encampment of the nations, who, having peacefully flocked there over night, wait till the Rue St. Honoré shall run out and greet them. It surprises me, sometimes, that those pretending to civilization are content to remain at a distance. What experience have they of life, — not to mention gayety and pleasure, but of the great purpose of life, — society? Man evidently is gregarious; Fourier's fables are founded on fact; we are nothing without our opposites, our fellows, our lights and shadows, colors, relations, combinations, our point d'appui, and our angle of sight. An isolated man is immensurable; he is also unpicturesque, unnatural, untrue. He is no longer the lord of Nature, animal and vegetable, — but Nature is the lord of him; the trees, skies, flowers, predominate, and he is in as bad taste as green and blue, or as an oyster in a vase of roses. The race swings naturally to clusters. It being admitted, then, that society is our normal state, where is it to be obtained in such perfection as at Paris? Show me the urbanity, the generosity in trifles, better than sacrifice, the incuriousness and freedom, the grace, and wit, and honor, that will equal such as I find here. Morality, — we were not speaking of it, — the intrusion is unnecessary; must that word with Anglo-Saxon pertinacity dog us round the world? A hollow mask, which Vice now and then lifts for a breath of air, I grant you this state may be called; but since I find the vice elsewhere, countenance my preference for the accompanying mask. But even this is vanishing; such drawing-rooms as Mme. de St. Cyr's are less and less frequent. Yet, though the delightful spell of the last century daily dissipates itself, and we are not now what we were twenty years ago, still Paris is, and will be to the end of time, for a cosmopolitan, the pivot on which the world revolves.

It was, then, as I have said, the day of Mme. de St. Cyr's dinner. Punctually at the hour, I presented myself, — for I have always esteemed it the least courtesy which a guest can render, that he should not cool his hostess's dinner.

The usual choice company waited. There was the Marquis of G., the ambassador from home; Col. Leigh, an attaché of that embassy; the Spanish and Belgian ministers; — all of whom, with myself, completed a diplomatic circle. There were also wits and artists, but no ladies whose beauty exceeded that of the St. Cyrs. With nearly all of this assemblage I held certain relations, so that I was immediately at ease. G. was the only one whom, perhaps, I would rather not have met, although we were the best of friends. They awaited but one, the Baron Stahl. Meanwhile Delphine stood coolly taking the measurement of the Marquis of G., while her mother entertained one and another guest with a low-toned flattery, gentle interest, or lively narration, as the case might demand.

In a country where a coup d'état was as easily given as a box on the ear, we all attentively watched for the arrival of one who had been sent from a neighboring empire to negotiate a loan for the tottering throne of this. Nor was expectation kept long on guard. In a moment, "His Excellency, the Baron Stahl!" was announced.

The exaggeration of his low bow to Mme. de St. Cyr, the gleam askance of his black eye, the absurd simplicity of his dress, did not particularly please me. A low forehead, straight black brows, a beardless cheek with a fine color which give him a fictitiously youthful appearance, were the most striking traits of his face; his person was not to be found fault with; but he boldly evinced his admiration for Delphine, and with a wicked eye.

As we were introduced, he assured me, in pure English, that he had pleasure in making the acquaintance of a gentleman whose services were so distinguished.

I, in turn, assured him of my pleasure in meeting a gentleman who appreciated them.

I had arrived at the house of Mme. de St. Cyr with a load on my mind, which for four weeks had weighed there; but before I thus spoke, it was lifted and gone. I had seen the Baron Stahl before, although not previously aware of it; and now, as he bowed, talked my native tongue so smoothly, drew a glove over the handsome hand upon whose first finger shone the only incongruity of his attire, a broad gold ring, holding a gaudy red stone, — as he stood smiling and expectant before me, a sudden chain of events flashed through my mind, an instantaneous heat, like lightning, welded them into logic. A great problem was resolved. For a second, the breath seemed snatched from my lips; the next, a lighter, freer man never trod in diplomatic shoes.

I really beg your pardon, — but perhaps from long usage, it has become impossible for me to tell a straight story. It is absolutely necessary to inform you of events already transpired.

In the first place, then, I, at this time, possessed a valet, the pink of valets, an Englishman, — and not the less valuable to me in a foreign capital, that, notwithstanding his long residence, he was utterly unable to speak one word of French intelligibly. Reading and writing it readily, his thick tongue could master scarcely a syllable. The adroitness and perfection with which he performed the duties of his place were unsurpassable. To a certain extent I was obliged to admit him into my confidence; I was not at all in his. In dexterity and despatch he equalled the advertisements. He never condescended to don my cast-off apparel, but, disposing of it, always arrayed himself in plain but gentlemanly garments. These do not complete the list of Hay's capabilities. He speculated. Respectable tenements in London called him landlord; in the funds certain sums lay subject to his order; to a profitable farm in Hants he contemplated future retirement; and passing upon the Bourse, I have received a grave bow, and have left him in conversation with an eminent capitalist respecting consols, drafts, exchange, and other erudite mysteries, where I yet find myself in the A B C. Thus not only was my valet a free-born Briton, but a landed proprietor. If the Rothschilds blacked your boots or shaved your chin, your emotions might be akin to mine. When this man, who had an interest in the India traders, brought the hot water into my dressing-room, of a morning, the Antipodes were tributary to me. To what extent might any little irascibility of mine drive a depression in the market! and I knew, as he brushed my hat, whether stocks rose or fell. In one respect, I was essentially like our Saxon ancestors, — my servant was a villain. If I had been merely a civilian, in any purely private capacity, having leisure to attend to personal concerns in the midst of the delicate specialties intrusted to me from the cabinet at home, the possession of so inestimable a valet might have bullied me beyond endurance. As it was, I found it rather agreeable than otherwise. He was tacitly my secretary of finance.

Several years ago, a diamond of wonderful size and beauty, having wandered from the East, fell into certain imperial coffers among our Continental neighbors; and at the same time some extraordinary intelligence, essential to the existence, so to speak, of that government, reached a person there who fixed as its price this diamond. After a while he obtained it, but, judging that prudence lay in departure, took it to England, where it was purchased for an enormous sum by the Duke of — as he will remain an unknown quantity, let us say X.

There are probably not a dozen such diamonds in the world, — certainly not three in England. It rejoiced in such flowery appellatives as the Sea of Splendor, the Moon of Milk; and, of course, those who had but parted with it under protest, as it were, determined to obtain it again at all hazards; — they were never famous for scrupulosity The Duke of X. was aware of this, and, for a time, the gem had lain idle, its glory muffled in a casket; but finally, on some grand occasion a few months prior to the period of which I have spoken above, it was determined to set it in the Duchess's coronet. Accordingly, one day, it was given by her son, the Marquis of G., into the hands of their solicitor, who should deliver it to her Grace's jeweller. It lay in a small shagreen case, and before the Marquis left, the solicitor placed the case in a flat leathern box, where lay a chain of most singular workmanship, the clasp of which was deranged. This chain was very broad, of a style known as the brickwork, but every brick was a tiny gem, set in a delicate filagree linked with the next, and the whole rainbowed lustrousness moving at your will, like the scales of some gorgeous Egyptian serpent; — the solicitor was to take this also to the jeweller. Having laid the box in his private desk, Ulster, his confidential clerk, locked it, while he bowed the Marquis down. Returning immediately, the solicitor took the flat box and drove to the jeweller's. He found the latter so crowded with customers, it being the fashionable hour, as to be unable to attend to him; he, however, took the solicitor into his inner room, a dark fire-proof place, and there quickly deposited the box within a safe, which stood inside

another, like a Japanese puzzle, and the solicitor, seeing
the doors double-locked and secured, departed; the other
promising to attend to the matter on the morrow.

Early the next morning, the jeweller entered his
dark room, and proceeded to unlock the safe. This being
concluded, and the inner one also thrown open, he
found the box in a last and entirely, as he had always
believed, secret compartment. Anxious to see this
wonder, this Eye of Morning, and Heart of Day, he
eagerly loosened the band and unclosed the box. It was
empty. There was no chain there; the diamond was
missing. The sweat streamed from his forehead, his
clothes were saturated, he believed himself the victim of
a delusion. Calling an assistant, every article and nook in
the dark room was examined. At last, in an extremity of
despair, he sent for the solicitor, who arrived in a breath.
The jeweller's alarm hardly equalled that of the other. In
his sudden dismay, he at first forgot the circumstances
and dates relating to the affair; afterward was doubtful.
The Marquis of G. was summoned, the police called in,
the jeweller given into custody. Every breath the solicitor
continued to draw only built up his ruin. He swallowed
laudanum, but, by making it an overdose, frustrated his
own design. He was assured, on his recovery, that no
suspicion attached to him. The jeweller now asseverated
that the diamond had never been given to him; but
though the jeweller had committed perjury, this was,
nevertheless, strictly true. Of course, whoever had the
stone would not attempt to dispose of it at present, and,
though communications were opened with the general

European police, there was very little to work upon. But by means of this last step the former possessors became aware of its loss, and I make no doubt had their agents abroad immediately.

Meanwhile, the case hung here, complicated and tantalizing, when one morning I woke in London. No sooner had G. heard of my arrival than he called, and, relating the affair, requested my assistance. I confess myself to have been interested, — foolishly so, I thought afterward; but we all have our weaknesses, and diamonds were mine. In company with the Marquis, I waited upon the solicitor, who entered into the few details minutely, calling frequently upon Ulster, a young, fresh-looking man, for corroboration. We then drove to the jeweller's new quarters, took him, under charge of the officers, to his place of business, where he nervously showed me every point that could bear upon the subject, and ended by exclaiming, that he was ruined, and all for a stone he had never seen. I sat quietly for a few moments. It stood, then, thus: — G. had given the thing to the solicitor, seen it put into the box, seen the box put into the desk; but while the confidential clerk, Ulster, locked the desk, the solicitor waited on the Marquis to the door, — returning, took the box, without opening it again, to the jeweller, who, in the hurry, shut it up in his safe, also without opening it. The case was perfectly clear. These mysterious things are always so simple! You know now as well as I, who took the diamond.

I did not choose to volunteer, but assented, on being desired. The police and I were old friends; they had so often assisted me, that I was not afraid to pay them in kind, and accordingly agreed to take charge of the case, still retaining their aid, should I require it. The jeweller was now restored to his occupation, although still subjected to a rigid surveillance, and I instituted inquiries into the recent movements of the young man Ulster. The case seemed to me to have been very blindly conducted. But, though all that was brought to light concerning him in London was perfectly fair and aboveboard, it was discovered that, not long since, he had visited Paris, — on the solicitor's business, of course, but gaining thereby an opportunity to transact any little affairs of his own. This was fortunate; for if any one could do anything in Paris, it was myself.

It is not often that I act as a detective. But one homogeneous to every situation could hardly play a pleasanter part for once. I have thought that our great masters in theory and practice, Machiavel and Talleyrand, were hardly more, on a large scale.

I was about to return to Paris, but resolved to call previously on the solicitor again. He welcomed me warmly, although my suspicions had not been imparted to him, and, with a more cheerful heart than had lately been habitual to him, entered into an animated conversation respecting the great case of Biter v. Bit, then absorbing so much of the public attention, frequently addressing Ulster, whose remarks were always pertinent, brief, and clear. As I sat actively discussing the topic, feeling no more interest in it than in the end of that cigar I just cut off, and noting exactly every look and motion of the unfortunate youth, I recollect the curious sentiment that filled me regarding him. What injury had he done me, that I should pursue him with punishment? Me? I am, and every individual is, integral with the commonwealth. It was the commonwealth he had injured. Yet, even then, why was I the one to administer justice? Why not continue with my coffee in the morning, my kings and cabinets and national chess at noon, my opera at night, and let the poor devil go? Why, but that justice is brought home to every member of society, — that naked duty requires no shirking of such responsibility, — that, had I failed here, the crime might, with reason, lie at my door and multiply, the criminal increase himself?

Very possibly you will not unite with me; but these little catechisms are, once in a while, indispensable, to vindicate one's course to one's self.

This Ulster was a handsome youth; — the rogues have generally all the good looks. There was nothing else remarkable about him but his quickness; he was perpetually on the alert; by constant activity, the rust was never allowed to collect on his faculties; his sharpness was distressing, — he appeared subject to a tense strain. Now his quill scratched over the paper unconcernedly, while he could join as easily in his master's conversation: nothing seemed to preoccupy him, or he held a mind open at every point. It is pitiful to remember him that morning, sitting quiet, unconscious, and free, utterly in the hands of that mighty Inquisition, the Metropolitan Police, with its countless arms, its cells and myrmidons in the remotest corners of the Continent, — at the mercy of so merciless a monster, and momently closer involved, like some poor prey round which a spider spins its bewildering web. It was also curious to observe the sudden suspicion that darkened his face at some innocent remark, — the quick shrinking and intrenched retirement, the manifest sting and rancor, as I touched his wound with a swift flash of my slender weapon and sheathed it again, and, after the thrust, the espionage, and the relief at believing it accidental. He had many threads to gather up and hold; — little electric warnings along them must have been constantly shocking him. He did that part well enough; it was a mistake, to begin with; he needed prudence. At that time I owed this Ulster nothing; now, however, I owe him a grudge, for some of the most harassing hours of my life were occasioned me by him. But I shall not cherish enmity on that account. With so promising a beginning, he will graduate and take his degree from the loftiest altitude in his line. Hemp is a narcotic; let it bring me forgetfulness.

In Paris I found it not difficult to trace such a person, since he was both foreign and unaccustomed. It was ascertained that he had posted several letters. A person of his description had been seen to drop a letter, the superscription of which had been read by one who picked it up for him. This superscription was the address of the very person who was likely to be the agent of the former possessors of the diamond, and had attracted attention. After all, — you know the Secret Force, — it was not so impossible to imagine what this letter contained, despite of its cipher. Such a person also had been met among the Jews, and at certain shops whose reputation was not of the clearest. He had called once or twice on Mme. de St. Cyr, on business relative to a vineyard adjoining her chateau in the Gironde, which she had sold to a wine merchant of England. I found a zest in the affair, as I pursued it.

We were now fairly at sea, but before long I found we were likely to remain there; in fact, nothing of consequence eventuated. I began to regret having taken the affair from the hands in which I had found it, and one day, it being a gala or some insatiable saint's day, I was riding, perplexed with that and other matters, and paying small attention to the passing crowd. I was vexed and mortified, and had fully decided to throw up the whole, — on such hairs do things hang, — when, suddenly turning a corner, my bridle-reins became entangled in the snaffle of another rider. I loosened them abstractedly, and not till it was necessary to bow to my strange antagonist on parting, did I glance up. The person before me was evidently not accustomed to play the dandy; he wore his clothes ill, sat his horse worse, and was uneasy in the saddle. The unmistakable air of the gamin was apparent beneath the superficies of the gentleman. Conspicuous on his costume, and wound like an order of merit upon his breast, glittered a chain, the chain, — each tiny brick-like gem spiked with a hundred sparks, and building a fabric of sturdy probabilities with the celerity of the genii in constructing Aladdin's palace. There, a cable to haul up the treasure, was the chain; — where was the diamond? I need not tell you how I followed this young friend, with what assiduity I kept him in sight, up and down, all day long, till, weary at last of his fine sport, as I certainly was of mine, he left his steed in stall and fared on his way a-foot. Still pursuing, now I threaded quay and square, street and alley, till he disappeared in a small shop, in one of those dark crowded lanes leading eastward from the Pont Neuf, in the city. It was the sign of a marchand des armures, and having provided myself with those persuasive arguments, a sergent-de-ville and a gendarme, I entered.

A place more characteristic it would be impossible to find. Here were piled bows of every material, ash, and horn, and tougher fibres, with slackened strings, and among them peered a rusty clarion and battle-axe, while the quivers that should have accompanied lay in a distant corner, their arrows serving to pin long, dusty, torn banners to the wall. Opposite the entrance, an archer in bronze hung on tiptoe, and levelled a steel bow, whose piercing fleche seemed sparkling with impatience to spring from his finger and flesh itself in the heart of the intruder. The hauberk and halberd, lance and casque, arquebuse and sword, were suspended in friendly congeries; and fragments of costly stuff swept from ceiling to floor, crushed and soiled by the heaps of rusty firelocks, cutlasses, and gauntlets thrown upon them. In one place, a little antique bust was half hid in the folds of some pennon, still dyed with battle-stains; in another, scattered treasures of Dresden and Sevres brought the drawing-room into the campaign; and all around bivouacked rifles, whose polished barrels glittered full of death, — pistols, variously mounted, for an insurgent at the barricades, or for a lost millionnaire at the gaming-table, — foils, with buttoned bluntness, — and rapiers whose even edges were viewless as if filed into air. Destruction lay everywhere, at the command of the owner of this place, and, had he possessed a particle of vivacity, it would have been hazardous to bow beneath his doorway. It did not, I must say, look like a place where I should find a diamond. As the owner came forward, I determined on my plan of action.

"You have, sir," I said, handing him a bit of paper, on which were scrawled some numbers, "a diamond in your possession, of such and so many carats, size, and value, belonging to the Duke of X., and left with you by an Englishman, Mr. Arthur Ulster. You will deliver it to me, if you please."

"Monsieur!" exclaimed the man, lifting his hands, and surveying me with the widest eyes I ever saw. "A diamond! In my possession! So immense a thing! It is impossible. I have not even seen one of the kind. It is a mistake. Jacques Noailles, the vender of jewels en gros, second door below, must be the man. One should perceive that my business is with arms, not diamonds. I have it not; it would ruin me."

Here he paused for a reply, but, meeting none, resumed. "M. Arthur Ulster! — I have heard of no such person. I never spoke with an Englishman. Bah! I detest them! I have no dealings with them. I repeat, I have not your jewel. Do you wish anything more of me?"

His vehemence only convinced me of the truth of my suspicions.

"These heroics are out of place," I answered. "I demand the article in question."

"Monsieur doubts me?" he asked, with a rueful face, — "questions my word, which is incontrovertible?" Here he clapped his hand upon a couteau-de-chasse lying near, but, appearing to think better of it, drew himself up, and, with a shower of nods flung at me, added, "I deny your accusation!" I had not accused him.

"You are at too much pains to convict yourself. I charge you with nothing," I said. "But this diamond must be surrendered."

"Monsieur is mad!" he exclaimed, "mad! he dreams! Do I look like one who possesses such a trophy? Does my shop resemble a mine? Look about! See! All that is here would not bring a hundredth part of its price. I beseech Monsieur to believe me; he has mistaken the number, or has been misinformed."

"We waste words. I know this diamond is here, as well as a costly chain — "

"On my soul, on my life, on my honor," he cried clasping his hands and turning up his eyes, "there is here nothing of the kind. I do not deal in gems. A little silk, a few weapons, a curiosity, a nicknack, comprise my stock. I have not the diamond. I do not know the thing. I am poor. I am honest. Suspicion destroys me!"

"As you will find, should I be longer troubled by your denials."

He was inflexible, and, having exhausted every artifice of innocence, wiped the tears from his eyes, — oh, these French! life is their theatre, — and remained quiet. It was getting dark. There was no gas in the place; but in the pause a distant street-lamp swung its light dimly round.

"Unless one desires to purchase, allow me to say that it is my hour for closing," he remarked, blandly, rubbing his black-bearded chin.

"My time is valuable," I returned. "It is late and dark. When your shop-boy lights up — "

"Pardon, — we do not light."

"Permit me, then, to perform that office for you. In this blaze you may perceive my companions, whom you have not appeared to recognize."

So saying, I scratched a match upon the floor, and, as the sergent-de-ville and the gendarme advanced, threw the light of the blue spirit of sulphurous flame upon them. In a moment more the match went out, and we remained in the demi-twilight of the distant lantern. The marchand des armures stood petrified and aghast. Had he seen the imps of Satan in that instant, it could have had no greater effect.

"You have seen them?" I asked. "I regret to inconvenience you; but unless this diamond is produced at once, my friends will put their seal on your goods, your property will be confiscated, yourself in a dungeon. In other words, I allow you five minutes; at the close of that time you will have chosen between restitution and ruin."

He remained apparently lost in thought. He was a big, stout man, and with one blow his powerful fist could easily have settled me. It was the last thing in his mind. At length he lifted his head, — "Rosalie!" he called.

At the word, a light foot pattered along a stone floor within, and in a moment a little woman stood in an arch raised by two steps from our own level. Carrying a candle, she descended and tripped toward him. She was not pretty, but sprightly and keen, as the perpetual attrition of life must needs make her, and wore the everlasting grisette costume, which displays the neatest of ankles, and whose cap is more becoming than wreaths of garden millinery. I am too minute, I see, but it is second nature. The two commenced a vigorous whispering amid sundry gestures and glances. Suddenly the woman turned, and, laying the prettiest of little hands on my sleeve, said, with a winning smile, —

"Is it a crime of lèse-majesté?"

This was a new idea, but might be useful.

"Not yet," I said; "two minutes more, and I will not answer for the consequence.'

Other whispers ensued.

"Monsieur," said the man, leaning on one arm over the counter, and looking up in my face, with the most engaging frankness, — "it is true that I have such a diamond; but it is not mine. It is left with me to be delivered to the Baron Stahl, who comes as an agent from his court for its purchase."

"Yes, — I know."

"He was to have paid me half a million francs, — not half its worth, — in trust for the person who left it, who is not M. Arthur Ulster, but Mme. de St. Cyr."

Madame de St. Cyr! How under the sun — No, — it could not be possible. The case stood as it stood before. The rogue was in deeper water than I had thought; he had merely employed Mme. de St. Cyr. I ran this over in my mind, while I said, "Yes."

"Now, sir," I continued, "you will state the terms of this transaction."

"With pleasure. For my trouble I was myself to receive patronage and five thousand francs. The Baron is to be here directly, on other and public business. Reine du ciel, Monsieur! how shall I meet him?"

"He is powerless in Paris; your fear is idle."

"True. There were no other terms."

"Nor papers?"

"The lady thought it safest to be without them. She took merely my receipt, which the Baron Stahl will bring to me from her before receiving this."

"I will trouble you for it now."

He bowed and shuffled away. At a glance from me, the gendarme slipped to the rear of the building, where three others were stationed at the two exits in that direction, to caution them of the critical moment, and returned. Ten minutes passed, — the merchant did not appear. If, after all, he had made off with it! There had been the click of a bolt, the half-stifled rattle of arms, as if a door had been opened and rapidly closed again, but nothing more.

"I will see what detains my friend," said Mademoiselle, the little woman.

We suffered her to withdraw. In a moment more a quick expostulation was to be heard.

"They are there, the gendarmes, my little one! I should have run, but they caught me, the villains! and replaced me in the house. Oh, sacre!" — and rolling this word between his teeth, he came down and laid a little box on the counter. I opened it. There was within a large, glittering, curiously cut piece of glass. I threw it aside.

"The diamond!" I exclaimed.

"Monsieur had it," he replied, stooping to pick up the glass with every appearance of surprise and care.

"Do you mean to say you endeavored to escape with that bawble? Produce the diamond instantly, or you shall hang as high as Haman!" I roared.

Whether he knew the individual in question or not, the threat was efficient; he trembled and hesitated, and finally drew the identical shagreen case from his bosom.

"I but jested," he said. "Monsieur will witness that I relinquish it with reluctance."

"I will witness that you receive stolen goods!" I cried, in wrath.

He placed it in my hands.

"Oh!" he groaned, from the bottom of his heart, hanging his head, and laying both hands on the counter before him, — "it pains, it grieves me to part with it!"

"And the chain," I said.

"Monsieur did not demand that!"

"I demand it now."

In a moment, the chain also was given me.

"And now will Monsieur do me a favor? Will he inform me by what means he ascertained these facts?"

I glanced at the garcon, who had probably supplied himself with his masters finery illicitly; — he was the means; — we have some generosity; — I thought I should prefer doing him the favor, and declined.

I unclasped the shagreen case; the sergent-de-ville and the gendarme stole up and looked over my shoulder; the garcon drew near with round eyes; the little woman peeped across; the merchant, with tears streaming over his face, gazed as if it had been a loadstone; finally, I looked myself. There it lay, the glowing, resplendent thing! flashing in affluence of splendor, throbbing and palpitant with life, drawing all the light from the little woman's candle, from the sparkling armor around, from the steel barbs, and the distant lantern, into its bosom. It was scarcely so large as I had expected to see it, but more brilliant than anything I could conceive of. I do not believe there is another such in the world. One saw clearly that the Oriental superstition of the sex of stones was no fable; this was essentially the female of diamonds, the queen herself, the principle of life, the rejoicing receptive force. It was not radiant, as the term literally taken implies; it seemed rather to retain its wealth, — instead of emitting its glorious rays, to curl them back like the fringe of a madrepore, and lie there with redoubled quivering scintillations, a mass of white magnificence, not prismatic, but a vast milky lustre. I closed the case; on reopening it, I could scarcely believe that the beautiful sleepless eye would again flash upon me. I did not comprehend how it could afford such perpetual richness, such sheets of lustre.

At last we compelled ourselves to be satisfied. I left the shop, dismissed my attendants, and, fresh from the contemplation of this miracle, again trod the dirty, reeking streets, crossed the bridge, with its lights, its warehouses midway, its living torrents who poured on unconscious of the beauty within their reach. The thought of their ignorance of the treasure, not a dozen yards distant, has often made me question if we all are not equally unaware of other and greater processes of life, of more perfect, sublimed and, as it were, spiritual crystallizations going on invisibly about us. But had these been told of the thing clutched in the hand of a passer, how many of them would have know where to turn? and we, — are we any better?

II

FOR a few days I carried the diamond about my person, and did not mention its recovery even to my valet, who knew that I sought it, but communicated only with the Marquis of G., who replied, that he would be in Paris on a certain day, when I could safely deliver it to him.

It was now generally rumored that the neighboring government was about to send us the Baron Stahl, ambassador concerning arrangements for a loan to maintain the sinking monarchy in supremacy at Paris, the usual synecdoche for France.

The weather being fine, I proceeded to call on Mme. de St. Cyr. She received me in her boudoir, and on my way thither I could not but observe the perfect quiet and cloistered seclusion that prevaded the whole house, — the house itself seeming only an adjunct of the still and sunny garden, of which one caught a glimpse through the long open hall- windows beyond. This boudoir did not differ from others to which I have been admitted: the same delicate shades; all the dainty appliances of Art for beauty; the lavish profusion of bijouterie; and the usual statuettes of innocence, to indicate, perhaps, the presence of that commodity which might not be guessed at otherwise; and burning in a silver cup, a rich perfume loaded the air with voluptuous sweetness. Through a half-open door an inner boudoir was to be seen, which must have been Delphine's; it looked like her; the prevailing hue was a soft purple, or gray; a prie-dieu, a bookshelf, and desk, of a dark West Indian wood, were just visible. There was but one picture, — a sad-eyed, beautiful Fate. It was the type of her nation. I think she worshipped it. And how apt is misfortune to degenerate into Fate! — not that the girl had ever experienced the former, but, dissatisfied with life, and seeing no outlet, she accepted it stoically and waited till it should be over. She needed to be aroused; — the station of an ambassadrice, which I desired for her, might kindle the spark. There were no flowers, no perfumes, no busts, in this ascetic place. Delphine herself, in some faint rosy gauze, her fair hair streaming round her, as she lay on a white-draped couch, half-risen on one arm, while she read the morning's feuilleton, was the most perfect statuary of which a room could boast, — illumined, as I saw her, by the gay beams that entered at the loftily-arched window, broken only by the flickering of the vine-leaves that clustered the curiously-latticed panes without. She resembled in kind a Nymph, just bursting from the sea; so Pallas might have posed for Aphrodite. Madame de St. Cyr received me with empressement, and, so doing, closed the door of this shrine. We spoke of various things, — of the court, the theatre, the weather, the world, — skating lightly round the slender edges of her secret, till finally she invited me to lunch with her in the garden. Here, on a rustic table, stood wine and a few delicacies, — while, by extending a hand, we could grasp the hanging pears and nectarines, still warm to the lip and luscious with sunshine, as we disputed possession with the envious wasp who had established a priority of claim.

"It is to be hoped," I said, sipping the Haut-Brion, whose fine and brittle smack contrasted rarely with the delicious juiciness of the fruit, "that you have laid in a supply of this treasure that neither moth nor rust doth corrupt, before parting with that little gem in the Gironde."

"Ah? You know, then, that I have sold it?"

"Yes," I replied. "I have the pleasure of Mr. Ulster's acquaintance."

"He arranged the terms for me," she said, with restraint, — adding, "I could almost wish now that it had not been."

This was probably true; for the sum which she hoped to receive from Ulster for standing sponsor to his jewel was possibly equal to the price of her vineyard.

"It was indispensable at the time, this sale; I thought best to hazard it on one more season. — If, after such advantages, Delphine will not marry, why — it remains to retire into the country and end our days with the barbarians!" she continued, shrugging her shoulders; "I have a house there."

"But you will not be obliged to throw us all into despair by such a step now," I replied.

She looked quickly, as if to see how nearly I had approached her citadel, — then, finding in my face no expression but a complimentary one, "No," she said, "I hope that my affairs have brightened a little. One never knows what is in store."

Before long I had assured myself that Mme. de St. Cyr was not a party to the theft, but had merely been hired by Ulster, who, discovering the state of her affairs, had not, therefore, revealed his own, — and this without in the least implying any knowledge on my part of the transaction. Ulster must have seen the necessity of leaving the business in the hands of a competent person, and Mme. de St. Cyr's financial talent was patent. There were few ladies in Paris who would have rejected the opportunity. Of these things I felt a tolerable certainty.

"We throng with foreigners," said Madame, archly, as I reached this point. "Diplomates, too. The Baron Stahl arrives in a day."

"I have heard," I responded. "You are acquainted?"

"Alas! no," she said. "I knew his father well, though he himself is not young. Indeed, the families thought once of intermarriage. But nothing has been said on the subject for many years. His Excellency, I hear, will strengthen himself at home by an alliance with the young Countess, the natural daughter of the Emperor."

"He surely will never be so imprudent as to rivet his chain by such a link!"

"It is impossible to compute the dice in those despotic countries," she rejoined, — which was pretty well, considering the freedom enjoyed by France at that period.

"It may be," I suggested, "that the Baron hopes to open this delicate subject with you yourself, Madame."

"It is unlikely," she said, sighing. "And for Delphine, should I tell her his excellency preferred scarlet, she would infallibly wear blue. Imagine her, Monsieur, in fine scarlet, with a scarf of gold gauze, and rustling grasses in that unruly gold hair of hers! She would be divine!"

The maternal instinct as we have it here at Paris confounds me. I do not comprehend it. Here was a mother who did not particularly love her child, who would not be inconsolable at her loss, would not ruin her own complexion by care of her during illness, would send her through fire and water and every torture to secure or maintain a desirable rank, who yet would entangle herself deeply in intrigue, would not hesitate to tarnish her own reputation, and would, in fact, raise heaven and earth to — endow this child with a brilliant match. And Mme. de St. Cyr seemed to regard Delphine, still further, as a cool matter of Art.

These little confidences, moreover, are provoking. They put you yourself so entirely out of the question.

"Mlle. de St. Cyr's beauty is peerless," I said, slightly chagrined, and at a loss. "If hearts were trumps, instead of diamonds!"

"We are poor," resumed Madame, pathetically. "Delphine is not an heiress. Delphine is proud. She will not stoop to charm. Her coquetry is that of an Amazon. Her kisses are arrows. She is Medusa!" And Madame, her mother, shivered.

Here, with her hair knotted up and secured by a tiny dagger, her gauzy drapery gathered in her arm, Delphine floated down the green alley toward us, as if in a rosy cloud. But this soft aspect never could have been more widely contradicted than by the stony repose and cutting calm of her beautiful face.

"The Marquis of G.," said her mother, "he also arrives ambassador. Has he talent? Is he brilliant? Wealthy, of course, — but gauche?"

Therewith I sketched for them the Marquis and his surroundings.

"It is charming," said Madame. "Delphine, do you attend?"

"And why?" asked Delphine, half concealing a yawn with her dazzling hand. "It is wearisome; it matters not to me."

"But he will not go to marry himself in France," said her mother. "Oh, these English," she added, with a laugh, "yourself, Monsieur, being proof of it, will not mingle blood, lest the Channel should still flow between the little red globules! You will go? but to return shortly? You will dine with me soon? Au revoir!" and she gave me her hand graciously, while Delphine bowed as if I were already gone, threw herself into a garden-chair, and commenced pouring the wine on a stone for a little tame snake which came out and lapped it.

Such women as Mme. de St. Cyr have a species of magnetism about them. It is difficult to retain one's self-respect before them, — for no other reason than that one is, at the moment, absorbed into their individuality, and thinks and acts with them. Delphine must have had a strong will, and perpetual antagonism did not weaken it. As for me, Madame had, doubtless, reasons of her own for tearing aside these customary bands of reserve — reasons which, if you do not perceive, I shall not enumerate.

III

"HAVE YOU MET WITH anything further in your search, sir?" asked my valet next morning.

"Oh, yes, Hay," I returned, in a very good humor, — "with great success. You have assisted me so much, that I am sure I owe it to you to say that I have found the diamond."

"Indeed, sir, you are very kind. I have been interested, but my assistance is not worth mentioning. I thought likely it might be, you appeared so quiet." — The cunning dog! — "How did you find it, sir, may I ask?"

I briefly related the leading facts, since he had been aware of the progress of the case to that point, — without, however, mentioning Mme. de St. Cyr's name.

"And Monsieur did not inform us!" a French valet would have cried.

"You were prudent not to mention it, sir," said Hay. "These walls must have better ears than ordinary; for a family has moved in on the first floor recently, whose actions are extremely suspicious. But is this precious affair to be seen?"

I took it from an inner pocket and displayed it, having discarded the shagreen case as inconvenient.

"His Excellency must return as he came," said I.

Hay's eyes sparkled.

"And do you carry it there, sir?" he asked, with surprise, as I restored it to my waistcoat-pocket.

"I shall take it to the bank," I said. "I do not like the responsibility."

"It is very unsafe," was the warning of this cautious fellow. "Why, sir! any of these swells, these pickpockets, might meet you, run against you, — so!" said Hay, suiting the action to the word," and, with the little sharp knife concealed in just such a ring as this I wear, give a light tap, and there's a slit in your vest sir, but no diamond!" — and instantly resuming his former respectful deportment, Hay handed me my gloves and stick, and smoothed my hat.

"Nonsense!" I replied, drawing on the gloves, "I should like to see the man who could be too quick for me. Any news from India, Hay?"

"None of consequence, sir. The indigo crop is said to have failed which advances the figure of that on hand, so that one or two fortunes will be made to-day. Your hat, sir? — your lunettes? Here they are, sir."

"Good morning, Hay."

"Good morning, sir."

I descended the stairs, buttoning my gloves, paused a moment at the door to look about, and proceeded down the street, which was not more than usually thronged. At the bank I paused to assure myself that the diamond was safe. My fingers caught in a singular slit. I started. As Hay had prophesied there was a fine longitudinal cut in my waistcoat, but the pocket was empty. My God! the thing was gone. I never can forget the blank nihility of all existence that dreadful moment when I stood fumbling for what was not. Calm as I sit here and tell of it, I vow to you a shiver courses through me at the very thought. I had circumvented Stahl only to destroy myself. The diamond was lost again. My mind flew like lightning over every chance, and a thousand started up like steel spikes to snatch the bolt. For a moment I was stunned, but, never being very subject to despair, on my recovery, which was almost at once, took every measure that could be devised. Who had touched me? Whom had I met? Through what streets had I come? In ten minutes the Prefect had the matter in hand. My injunctions were strict privacy. I sincerely hoped the mishap would not reach England; and if the diamond were not recovered before the Marquis of G. arrived, — why, there was the Seine. It is all very well to talk, — yet suicide is so French an affair, that an Englishman does not take to it naturally, and, except in November, the Seine is too cold and damp for comfort, but during that month I suppose it does not greatly differ in these respects from our own atmosphere.

A preternatural activity now possessed me. I slept none, ate little, worked immoderately. I spared no efforts, for everything was at stake. In the midst of all, G. arrived. Hay also exerted himself to the utmost; I promised him a hundred pounds, if I found it. He never told me that he said how it would be, never intruded the state of the market, never resented my irritating conduct, but watched me with narrow yet kind solicitude, and frequently offered valuable suggestions, which, however, as everything else did, led to nothing. I did not call on G., but in a week or so his card was brought up one morning to me. "Deny me," I groaned. It yet wanted a week of the day on which I had promised to deliver him the diamond Meanwhile the Baron Stahl had reached Paris, but he still remained in private, — few had seen him.

The police were forever on the wrong track. Today they stopped the old Comptesse du Quesne and her jewels, at the Barriere; to-morrow, with their long needles, they riddled a package of lace destined for the Duchess of X. herself; the Secret Service was doubled; and to crown all, a splendid new star of the testy Prince de Ligne was examined and proclaimed to be paste, — the Prince swearing vengeance, if he could discover the cause, — while half Paris must have been under arrest. My own hotel was ransacked thoroughly, — Hay begging that his traps might be included, — but nothing resulted, and I expected nothing, for, of course, I could swear that the stone was in my pocket when I stepped into the street. I confess I never was nearer madness, — every word and gesture stung me like asps, — I walked on burning coals. Enduring all this torment, I must yet meet my daily comrades, eat ices at Tortoni's, stroll on the Boulevards, call on my acquaintance, with the same equanimity as before. I believe I was equal to it. Only by contrast with that blessed time when Ulster and diamonds were unknown, could I imagine my past happiness, my present wretchedness. Rather than suffer it again, I would be stretched on the rack till ever! bone in my skin were broken. I cursed Mr. Arthur Ulster every hour in the day; myself, as well; and even now the word diamond sends a cold blast to my heart. I often met my friend the marchand des armures. It was his turn to triumph; I fancied there must be a hang-dog kind of air about me, as about every sharp man who has been outwitted. It wanted finally but two days of that on which I was to deliver the diamond.

One midnight, armed with a dark lantern and a cloak, I was traversing the streets alone, — unsuccessful, as usual, just now solitary, and almost in despair. As I turned a corner, two men were but scarcely visible a step before me. It was a badly-lighted part of the town. Unseen and noiseless I followed. They spoke in low tones, — almost whispers; or rather, one spoke, — the other seemed to nod assent.

"On the day but one after to-morrow," I heard spoken in English. Great Heavens! was it possible? had I arrived at a clew? That was the day of days for me. "You have given it, you say, in this billet, — I wish to be exact, you see," continued the voice, — "to prevent detection, you gave it, ten minutes after it came into your hands, to the butler of Madame ," (here the speaker stumbled on the rough pavement, and I lost the name,) "who," he continued, "will put it in the —" (a second stumble acted like a hiccough) "cellar."

"Wine-cellar," I thought; "and what then?"

"In the ——." A third stumble was followed by a round German oath. How easy it is for me now to fill up the little blanks which that unhappy pavement caused!

"You share your receipts with this butler. On the day I obtain it," he added, and I now perceived his foreign accent, "I hand you one hundred thousand francs; afterward, monthly payments till you have received the stipulated sum. But how will this butler know me, in season to prevent a mistake? Hem! — he might give it to the other!"

My hearing had been trained to such a degree that I would have promised to catch any given dialogue of the spirits themselves, but the whisper that answered him eluded me. I caught nothing but a faint sibillation. "Your ring?" was the rejoinder. "He shall be instructed to recognize it? Very well. It is too large, — no, that will do, it fits the first finger. There is nothing more. I am under infinite obligations, sir; they shall be remembered. Adieu!"

The two parted; which should I pursue? In desperation I turned my lantern upon one, and illumined a face fresh with color, whose black eyes sparkled askance after the retreating figure, under straight black brows. In a moment more he was lost in a false cul-de-sac, and I found it impossible to trace the other.

I was scarcely better off than before; but it seemed to me that I had obtained something, and that now it was wisest to work this vein. "The butler of Madame — —." There were hundreds of thousands of Madames in town. I might call on all, and he as old as the Wandering Jew at the last call. The cellar. Wine-cellar, of course, — that came by a natural connection with butler, — but whose? There was one under my own abode; certainly I would explore it. Meanwhile, let us see the entertainments for Wednesday. The Prefect had a list of these. For some I found I had cards; I determined to allot a fraction of time to as many as possible; my friends in the Secret Service would divide the labor. Among others, Madame de St. Cyr gave a dinner, and, as she had been in the affair, I determined not to neglect her on this occasion, although having no definite idea of what had been, or plan of what should be done. I decided not to speak of this occurrence to Hay, since it might only bring him off some trail that he had struck.

Having been provided with keys, early on the following evening I entered the wine-cellar, and, concealed in an empty cask that would have held a dozen of me, waited for something to turn up. Really, when I think of myself, a diplomate, a courtier, a man-about-town, curled in a dusty, musty wine-barrel, I am moved with vexation and laughter. Nothing, however, turned up, — and at length I retired baffled. The next night came, — no news, no identification of my black-browed man, no success; but I felt certain that something must transpire in that cellar. I don't know why I had pitched upon that one in particular, but, at an earlier hour than on the previous night, I again donned the cask. A long time must have elapsed; dead silence filled the spacious vaults, except where now and then some Sillery cracked the air with a quick explosion, or some newer wine bubbled round the bung of its barrel with a faint effervescence. I had no intention of leaving this place till morning, but it suddenly appeared like the most woeful waste of time. The master of this tremendous affair should be abroad and active; who knew what his keen eyes might detect; what loss his absence might occasion in this nick of time? And here he was, shut up and locked in a wine-cellar! I began to be very nervous; I had already, with aid, searched every crevice of the cellar; and now I thought it would be some consolation to discover the thief, if I never regained the diamond. A distant clock tolled midnight. There was a faint noise, — a mouse? — no, it was too prolonged; — nor did it sound like the fiz of Champagne; — a great iron door was turning on its hinges; a man with a lantern was entering; another followed, and another. They seated themselves. In a few moments, appearing one by one and at intervals, some thirty people were in the cellar. Were they all to share in the proceeds of the diamond? With what jaundiced eye we behold things! I myself saw all that was only through the lens of this diamond, of which not one of these men had ever heard. As the lantern threw its feeble glimmer on this group, and I surveyed them through my loophole, I thought I had never seen so wild and savage a picture, such enormous shadows, such bold outline, such a startling flash on the face of their leader, such light retreating up the threatening arches. More resolute brows, more determined words, more unshrinking hearts, I had not met. In fact, I found myself in the centre of a conspiracy, a society as vindictive as the Jacobins, as unknown and terrible as the Marianne of to-day. I was thunderstruck, too, at the countenances on which the light fell, — men the loyalest in estimation, ministers and senators, millionnaires who had no reason for discontent, dandies whose reason was supposed to be devoted to their tailors, poets and artists of generous aspiration and suspected tendencies, and one woman, — Delphine de St. Cyr. Their plans were brave, their determination lofty, their conclave serious and fine; yet as slowly they shut up their hopes and fears in the black masks, one man bent toward the lantern to adjust his. When he lifted his face before concealing it, I recognized him also. I had met him frequently at the Bureau of Police; he was, I believe, Secretary of the Secret Service.

I had no sympathy with these people. I had sufficient liberty myself, I was well enough satisfied with the world, I did not care to revolutionize France; but my heart rebelled at the mockery, as this traitor and spy, this creature of a system by which I gained my fame, showed his revolting face and veiled it again. And Delphine, what had she to do with them? One by one, as they entered, they withdrew, and I was left alone again. But all this was not my diamond.

Another hour elapsed. Again the door opened, and remained ajar. Some one entered, whom I could not see. There was a pause, — then a rustle, — the door creaked ever so little. "Art thou there?" lisped a shrill whisper, — a woman, as I could guess.

"My angel, it is I," was returned, a semitone lower. She approached, he advanced, and the consequence was a salute resonant as the smack with which a Dutch burggomaster may be supposed to set down his mug. I was prepared for anything. Ye gods! if it should be Delphine! But the base suspicion was birth-strangled as they spoke again. The conversation which now ensued between these lovers under difficulties was tender and affecting beyond expression. I had felt guilty enough when an unwilling auditor of the conspirators, — since, though one employs spies, one does not therefore act that part one's self, but on emergencies, — an unwillingness which would not, however, prevent my turning to advantage the information gained; but here, to listen to this rehearsal of woes and blisses, this ah mon Fernand, this aria in an area, growing momently more fervent, was too much I overturned the cask, scrambled upon my feet, and fled from the cellar leaving the astounded lovers to follow, while, agreeably to my instincts and regardless of the diamond, I escaped the embarrassing predicament.

At length it grew to be noon of the appointed day. Nothing had transpired; all our labor was idle. I felt, nevertheless, more buoyant than usual, — whether because I was now to put my fate to the test, or that today was the one of which my black-browed man had spoken, and I therefore entertained a presentiment of good fortune, I cannot say. But when, in unexceptionable toilet, I stood on Mme. de St. Cyr's steps, my heart sunk. G. was doubtless already within, and I thought of the marchand des armures' exclamation, "Queen of Heaven, Monsieur! how shall I meet him!" I was plunged at once into the profoundest gloom. Why had I undertaken the business at all? This interference, this good-humor, this readiness to oblige, — it would ruin me yet! I forswore it, as Falstaff forswore honor. Why needed I to meddle in the melee? Why — But I was no catechumen. Questions were useless now. My emotions are not chronicled on my face, I flatter myself; and with my usual repose I saluted our hostess. Greeting G. without any allusion to the diamond, the absence of which allusion he received as a point of etiquette, I was conversing with Mrs. Leigh, when the Baron Stahl was announced. I turned to look at his Excellency. A glance electrified me. There was my dark-browed man of the midnight streets. It must, then, have been concerning the diamond that I had heard him speak. His countenance, his eager glittering eye, told that to-day was as eventful to him as to me. If he were here, I could well afford to be. As he addressed me in English, my certainty was confirmed; and the instant in which I observed the ring, gaudy and coarse, upon his finger, made confirmation doubly sure. I own I was surprised that anything could induce the Baron to wear such an ornament. Here he was actually risking his reputation as a man of taste, as an exquisite, a leader of haut ton, a gentleman, by the detestable vulgarity of this ring. But why do I speak so of the trinket? Do I not owe it a thrill of as fine joy as I ever knew? Faith! it was not unfamiliar to me. It had been a daily sight for years. In meeting the Baron Stahl I had found the diamond.

The Baron Stahl was then, the thief? Not at all. My valet, as of course you have been all along aware, was the thief.

My valet, moreover, was my instructor; he taught me not again to scour Cathay for what might be lying under my hand at home. Nor have I since been so acute as to overreach myself. Yet I can explain such intolerable stupidity only by remembering that when one has been in the habit of pointing his telescope at the stars, he is not apt to turn it upon pebbles at his feet.

The Marquis of G. took down Mme. de St. Cyr; Stahl preceded me, with Delphine. As we sat at table, G. was at the right, I at the left of our hostess Next G. sat Delphine; below her, the Baron; so that we were nearly vis-à-vis. I was now as fully convinced that Mme. de St. Cyr's cellar was the one, as the day before I had been that the other was; I longed to reach it. Hay had given the stone to a butler — doubtless this — the moment of its theft; but, not being aware of Mme. de St. Cyr's previous share in the adventure, had probably not afforded her another. And thus I concluded her to be ignorant of the game we were about to play; and I imagined, with the interest that one carries into a romance, the little preliminary scene between the Baron and Madame that must have already taken place, being charmed by the cheerfulness with which she endured the loss of the promised reward.

As the Baron entered the dining-room, I saw him withdraw his glove, and move the jewelled hand across his hair while passing the solemn butler, who gave it a quick recognition; — the next moment we were seated. There were only wines on the table, clustered around a central ornament, — a bunch of tall silver rushes and flagleaves, on whose airy tip danced fleurs-de-lis of frosted silver, a design of Delphine's, — the dishes being on sidetables, from which the guests were served as they signified their choice of the variety on their cards. Our number not being large, and the custom so informal, rendered it pleasant.

I had just finished my oysters and was pouring out a glass of Chablis, when another plate was set before the Baron.

"His Excellency has no salt," murmured the butler, — at the same time placing one beside him. A glance, at entrance, had taught me that most of the service was uniform; this dainty little saliere I had noticed on the buffet, solitary, and unlike the others. What a fool had I been! Those gaps in the Baron's remarks caused by the pavingstones, how easily were they to be supplied!

"Madame?"

Madame de St. Cyr.

"The cellar?"

A salt-cellar.

How quick the flash that enlightened me while I surveyed the saliere!

"It is exquisite! Am I never to sit at your table but some new device charms me?" I exclaimed. "Is it your design, Mademoiselle?" I said, turning to Delphine.

Delphine, who had been ice to all the Baron's advances, only curled her lip. "Des babioles!" she said.

"Yes, indeed!" cried Mme. de St. Cyr, extending her hand for it. "But none the less her taste. Is it not a fairy thing? À Cellini! Observe this curve, these lines! but one man could have drawn them!" — and she held it for our scrutiny. It was a tiny hand and arm of ivory, parting the foam of a wave and holding a golden shell, in which the salt seemed to have crusted itself as if in some secretest ocean-hollow. I looked at the Baron a moment; his eyes were fastened upon the saliere, and all the color had forsaken his cheeks, — his face counted his years. The diamond was in that little shell. But how to obtain it? I had no novice to deal with; nothing but finesse would answer.

"Permit me to examine it?" I said. She passed it to her left hand for me to take. The butler made a step forward.

"Meanwhile, Madame," said the Baron, smiling, "I have no salt."

The instinct of hospitality prevailed; — she was about to return it. Might I do an awkward thing? Unhesitatingly. Reversing my glass, I gave my arm a wider sweep than necessary, and, as it met her hand with violence, the saliere fell. Before it touched the floor I caught it. There was still a pinch of salt left, — nothing more.

"A thousand pardons!" I said, and restored it to the Baron.

His Excellency beheld it with dismay; it was rare to see him bend over and scrutinize it with starting eyes.

"Do you find there what Count Arnaldos begs in the song," asked Delphine, — "the secret of the sea, Monsieur?"

He handed it to the butler, observing, "I find here no — "

"Salt, Monsieur?" replied the man, who did not doubt but all had gone right, and replenished it.

Had one told me in the morning, that no intricate manœuvres, but a simple blunder, would effect this, I might have met him in the Bois de Boulogne.

"We will not quarrel," said my neighbor, lightly, with reference to the popular superstition

"Rather propitiate the offended deities by a crumb tossed over the shoulder," added I.

"Over the left?" asked the Baron, to intimate his knowledge of another idiom, together with a reproof for my gauchene.

"A gauche, — quelquefois c'est justement a droit, " I replied.

"Salt in any pottage," said Madame, a little uneasily, "is like surprise in an individual; it brings out the flavor of every ingredient, so my cook tells me."

"It is a preventive of palsy," I remarked, as the slight trembling of my adversary's finger caught my eye.

"And I have noticed that a taste for it is peculiar to those who trace their blood," continued Madame.

"Let us, therefore, elect a deputation to those mines near Cracow," said Delphine.

"To our cousins, the slaves there?" laughed her mother.

"I must vote to lay your bill on the table, Mademoiselle," I rejoined.

"But with a boule blanche, Monsieur?"

"As the salt has been laid on the floor," said the Baron.

Meanwhile, as this light skirmishing proceeded, my sleeve and Mme. de St. Cyr's dress were slightly powdered, but I had not seen the diamond. The Baron, bolder than I, looked under the table, but made no discovery. I was on the point of dropping my napkin to accomplish a similar movement when my accommodating neighbor dropped hers. To restore it, I stooped. There it lay, large and glowing, the Sea of Splendor, the Moon of Milk, the Torment of my Life, on the carpet, within half an inch of a lady's slipper Mademoiselle de St. Cyr's foot had prevented the Baron from seeing it; now it moved and unconsciously covered it. All was as I wished. I hastily restored the napkin, and looked steadily at Delphine, — so steadily, that she perceived some meaning, as she had already suspected a game. By my sign she understood me, pressed her foot upon the stone and drew it nearer. In France we do not remain at table until unfit for a lady's society, — we rise with them. Delphine needed to drop neither napkin nor handkerchief; she composedly stooped and picked up the stone, so quickly at no one saw what it was.

"And the diamond?" said the Baron to the butler, rapidly, as he passed.

"It was in the saliere," whispered the astonished creature.

IV

IN THE DRAWING-ROOM I sought the Marquis.

"To-day I was to surrender you your property," I said; "it is here."

"Do you know," he replied, "I thought I must have been mistaken?"

"Any of our volatile friends here might have been," I resumed; "for us it is impossible. Concerning this, when you return to France, I will relate the incidents; at present, there are those who will not hesitate to take life to obtain its possession. A conveyance leaves in twenty minutes; and if I owned the diamond, it should not leave me behind. Moreover, who knows what a day may bring forth? To-morrow there may be an émeute. Let me restore the thing as you withdraw."

The Marquis, who is not, after all, the Lion of England, pausing a moment to transmit my words from his ear to his brain, did not afterward delay to make inquiries or adieux, but went to seek Mme. de St. Cyr and wish her good-night, on his departure from Paris. As I awaited his return, which I knew would not be immediate, Delphine left the Baron and joined me.

"You beckoned me?" she asked.

"No, I did not."

"Nevertheless, I come by your desire, I am sure."

"Mademoiselle," I said, "I am not in the custom of doing favors; I have forsworn them. But before you return me my jewel, I risk my head and render one last one, and to you."

"Do not, Monsieur, at such price," she responded, with a slight mocking motion of her hand.

"Delphine! those resolves, last night, in the cellar, were daring, the were noble, yet they were useless."

She had not started, but a slight tremor ran over her person and vanished while I spoke.

"They will be allowed to proceed no farther, — the axe is sharpened; for the last man who adjusted his mask was a spy, — was the Secretary of the Secret Service

Delphine could not have grown paler than was usual with her of late. She flashed her eye upon me.

"He was, it may be, Monsieur himself," she said.

"I do not claim the honor of that post."

"But you were there, nevertheless, — a spy!"

"Hush, Delphine! It would be absurd to quarrel. I was there for the recovery of this stone, having heard that it was in a cellar, — when, stupidly enough, I had insisted should be a wine-cellar."

"It was, then — "

"In a salt-cellar, — a blunder which, as you do not speak English, you cannot comprehend. I never mix with treason, and did not wish to assist at your pastimes. I speak now, that you may escape."

"If Monsieur betrays his friends, the police, why should I expect a kinder fate?"

"When I use the police, they are my servants, not my friends. I simply warn you, that, before sunrise, you will be safer travelling than sleeping, — safer next week in Vienna than in Paris."

"Thank you! And the intelligence is the price of the diamond? If I had not chanced to pick it up, my throat," and she clasped it with her fingers, "had been no slenderer than the others?"

"Delphine, will you remember, should you have occasion to do so in Vienna, that it is just possible for an Englishman to have affections, and sentiments, and, in fact, sensations? that, with him, friendship can be inviolate, and to betray it an impossibility? And even were it not, I, Mademoiselle have not the pleasure to be classed by you as a friend."

"You err. I esteem Monsieur highly."

I was impressed by her coolness.

"Let me see if you comprehend the matter," I demanded.

"Perfectly. The arrest will be used to-night, the guillotine tomorrow."

"You will take immediate measures for flight?"

"No, — I do not see that life has value. I shall be the debtor of him who takes it."

"A large debt. Delphine, I exact a promise of you. I do not care to have endangered myself for nothing. It is not ù worth while to make your mother unhappy. Life is not yours to throw away. I appeal to your magnanimity."

"'Affections, sentiments, sensations!'" she quoted. "Your own danger for the affection, — it is an affair of the heart! Mme. de St. Cyr's unhappiness, — there is the sentiment. You are angry, Monsieur, — that must be the sensation."

"Delphine, I am waiting."

"Ah, well. You have mentioned Vienna, — and why? Liberals are countenanced there?"

"Not in the least. But Madame l'Ambassadrice will be countenanced.'

"I do not know her."

"We are not apt to know ourselves."

"Monsieur, how idle are these cross-purposes!" she said, folding her fan.

"Delphine," I continued, taking the fan, "tell me frankly which of these two men you prefer, — the Marquis or his Excellency."

"The Marquis? He is antiphlogistic, — he is ice. Why should I freeze myself? I am frozen now, — I need fire!"

Her eyes burned as she spoke, and a faint red flushed her cheek.

"Mademoiselle, you demonstrate to me that life has yet a value to you."

"I find no fire," she said, as the flush fell away.

"The Baron?"

"I do not affect him."

"You will conquer your prejudice in Vienna."

"I do not comprehend you, Monsieur; — you speak in riddles, which I do not like."

"I will speak plainer. But first let me ask you for the diamond."

"The diamond? It is yours? How am I certified of it? I find it on the floor; you say it was in my mother's saliere; it is her affair, not mine. No, Monsieur, I do not see that the thing is yours."

Certainly there was nothing to be done but to relate the story, which I did, carefully omitting the Baron's name. At its conclusion, she placed the prize in my hand.

"Pardon, Monsieur." she said; "without doubt you should receive it. And this agent of the government, — one could turn him like hot iron in this vice, — who was he?"

"The Baron Stahl."

All this time G. had been waiting on thorns, and, leaving her now, I approached him, displayed for an instant the treasure on my palm, and slipped it into his. It was done. I bade farewell to this Eye of Morning and Heart of Day, this thing that had caused me such pain and perplexity and pleasure, with less envy and more joy than I thought myself capable of. The relief and buoyancy that seized me, as his hand closed upon it, I shall not attempt to portray. An abdicated king was not freer.

The Marquis departed, and I, wandering round the salon, was next stranded upon the Baron. He was yet hardly sure of himself. We talked indifferently for a few moments, and then I ventured on the great loan. He was, as became him, not communicative, but scarcely thought it would be arranged. I then spoke of Delphine.

"She is superb!" said the Baron, staring at her boldly.

She stood opposite, and, in her white attire on the background of the blue curtain, appeared like an impersonation of Greek genius relieved upon the blue of an Athenian heaven. Her severe and classic outline, her pallor, her downcast lids, her absorbed look, only heightened the resemblance. Her reverie seemed to end abruptly, the same red stained her cheek again, her lips curved in a proud smile, she raised her glowing eyes and observed us regarding her. At too great distance to hear our words, she quietly repaid our glances in the strength of her new decision, and then, turning, began to entertain those next her with an unwonted spirit.

"She has needed," I replied to the Baron, "but one thing, — to be aroused, to be kindled. See, it is done! I have thought that a life of cabinets and policy might achieve this, for her talent is second not even to her beauty."

"It is unhappy that both should be wasted," said the Baron. "She, of course, will never marry."

"Why not?"

"For various reasons."

"One?"

"She is poor."

"Which will not signify to your Excellency. Another?"

"She is too beautiful. One would fall in love with her. And to love one's own wife — it is ridiculous!"

"Who should know?" I asked.

"All the world would suspect and laugh."

"Let those laugh that win."

"No, — she would never do as a wife; but then as ____"

"But then in France we do not insult hospitality!"

The Baron transferred his gaze to me for a moment, then tapped his snuff-box, and approached the circle round Delphine.

It was odd that we, the arch enemies of the hour, could speak without the intervention of seconds; but I hoped that the Baron's conversation might be diverting, — the Baron hoped that mine might be didactic.

They were very gay with Delphine. He leaned on the back of a chair and listened. One spoke of the new gallery of the Tuileries, and the five pavilions, — a remark which led us to architecture.

"We all build our own houses," said Delphine, at last, "and then complain that they cramp us here, and the wind blows in there, while the fault is not in the order, but in us, who increase here and shrink there without reason."

"You speak in metaphors," said the Baron.

"Precisely. A truth is often more visible veiled than nude."

"We should soon exhaust the orders," I interposed; "for who builds like his neighbor?"

"Slight variations, Monsieur! Though we take such pains to conceal the style, it is not difficult to tell the order of architecture chosen by the builders in this room. My mother, for instance — you perceive that her pavilion would be the florid Gothic."

"Mademoiselle's is the Doric," I said.

"Has been," she murmured, with a quick glance.

"And mine, Mademoiselle?" asked the Baron, indifferently.

"Ah, Monsieur," she returned, looking serenely upon him, "when one has all the winning cards in hand and yet loses the stake, we allot him un pavillon chinois." — which was the polite way of dubbing him Court Fool.

The Baron's eyes fell. Vexation and alarm were visible on his contracted brow. He stood in meditation for some time. It must have been evident to him that Delphine knew of the recent occurrences, — that here in Paris she could denounce him as the agent of a felony, the participant of a theft. What might prevent it? Plainly but one thing: no woman would denounce her husband. He had scarcely contemplated this step on arrival.

The guests were again scattered in groups round the room. I examined an engraving on an adjacent table. Delphine reclined as lazily in a fauteuil as if her life did not hang in the balance. The Baron drew near.

"Mademoiselle," said he, "you allotted me just now a cap and bells. If two should wear it? — if I should invite another into my pavillon chinois? — if I should propose to complete an alliance, desired by my father, with the ancient family of St. Cyr? — if, in short, Mademoiselle, I should request you to become my wife?"

"Eh, bien, Monsieur, — and if you should?" I heard her coolly reply.

But it was no longer any business of mine. I rose and sought Mme. de St. Cyr, who, I thought, was slightly uneasy, perceiving some mystery to be afloat. After a few words, I retired.

Archimedes, as perhaps you have never heard, needed only a lever to move the world. Such a lever I had put into the hands of Delphine, with which she might move, not indeed the grand globe, with its multiplied attractions, relations, and affinities, but the lesser world of circumstances, of friends and enemies, the circle of hopes, fears, ambitions. There is no woman, as I believe, but could have used it.

V

THE NEXT DAY was scarcely so quiet in the city as usual. The great loan had not been negotiated. Both the Baron Stahl and the English minister had left Paris, — and there was a coup d'état.

But the Baron did not travel alone. There had been a ceremony at midnight in the Church of St. Sulpice, and her excellency the Baroness Stahl, nee de St. Cyr, accompanied him.

It is a good many years since. I have seen the diamond in the Duchess of X.'s coronet, once, when a young queen put on her royalty, — but I have never seen Delphine. The Marquis begged me to retain the chain, and I gave myself the pleasure of presenting it, through her mother, to the Baroness Stahl. I hear, that, whenever she desires to effect any cherished object which the Baron opposes, she has only to wear this chain, and effect it. It appears to possess a magical power, and its potent spell enslaves the Baron as the lamp and ring of Eastern tales enslaved the Afrites. The life she leads has aroused her. She is no longer the impassive Silence; she has found her fire. I hear of her as the charm of a brilliant court, as the soul of a nation of intrigue. Of her beauty one does not speak, but her talent is called prodigious. What impels me to ask the idle question, If it were well to save her life for this? Undoubtedly she fills a station which, in that empire, must be the summit of a woman's ambition. Delphine's Liberty was not a principle, but a dissatisfaction. The Baroness Stahl is vehement, is Imperialist, is successful. While she lives, it is on the top of the wave; when she dies — ah! what business has Death in such a world?

As I said, I have never seen Delphine since her marriage. The beautiful statuesque girl occupies a niche into which the blazing and magnificent intrigante cannot crowd. I do not wish to be disillusioned. She has read me a riddle, — Delphine is my Sphinx.

VI

AS FOR MR. HAY — I once said the Antipodes were tributary to me, not thinking that I should ever become tributary to the Antipodes. But such is the case; since, partly through my instrumentality, that enterprising individual has been located in their vicinity, where diamonds are not to be had for the asking, and the greatest rogue is not a Baron.

DARK WAYS

"Tortured with winter's storms, and tossed with a tumultuous sea."

WHEN God's curse forsook my country, it fell on me. I had been young and heroic; I had fought well; what portion of the clock-work of Fate had been allotted me I had utterly performed. Twelve years ago I became a man and strove for my country's freedom; now she has attained her heights without me, and I -- what am I? A shapeless hulk, that stays in the shadow, and that hates the world and the people of the world, and verily the God above the world!

"Fight!" whispered Father Anselmo, the young priest, to me, at my last shrift; and fight I did. For from Italy's bosom I had drawn the strength of sword-arm, hip, and thigh; and I vowed to lose that arm and life and all that made life dear toward the trampling of oppressors from the sacred place.

My sun rose in storm, it continued in storm, -- why not so have set? Why not have died when swords swept their lightnings about me, when the glorious thunders of battle rolled around and sulphurous blasts enveloped, when the air was full of the bray of bugle and beat of drum, of shout and shriek, exultation and agony? Why not have gone with the crowd of souls reeking with daring and desire? Why, oh, why thus left alone to wither? Why still hangs that sun above me, yet wrapt and veiled and utterly obscured in thick, murk mists of sorrow and despair?

Peace! -- let me tell you my story.

Since Father Anselmo -- like all youth, whether under cowl, cap, or crown -- was a Liberal at heart, I had not wanted counsel; but when I had told him all my yearnings and aspirations, had bared to him the throbbings of my very thought, and he had replied in that one blessed word, I hastened away. There were none to whom I should say farewell; I was alone in the world. This wild blood of my veins ran in no other veins; I knew thoroughly the wide freedom of solitude; the sins and the virtues of my race, whatever they were, had culminated in me. As I looked back, that morning, the castle, planted in a dimple of its demesnes, old and gray and watched by purple peaks of Apennine, seemed to hide its command only under the mask of silence. The wood through which I went, with its alluring depths, the moss verdant in everlasting spring beneath my eager feet, each bough I lifted, the blossoms that blew their gales after, the bearded grasses that shook in the wind, all gave me their secret sigh; all the sweet land around, the distant hill, the distant shore, said, "Redeem me from my chains!" I came across a sylvan statue, some faun nestled in the forest: the rains had stained, frosts cracked, suns blistered it; but what of those? A vine covered with thorns and stemmed with cords had wreathed about it and bound it closely in serpent-coils. I stayed and tore apart the fetters till my hands bled, cut away the twisting branches, and set the god free from his bonds. Triumph rose to my lips, for I said, "So will I free my country!" Ah, there was my error, -- the shackling vines would grow again, and infold the marble image that had consecrated the forest-glooms; there is the flaw in all my work, -- I have shorn, but have never uprooted an evil. Youth is a fool; the young Titans cannot scale heaven, -- heaven, that, if what I live through be true, is ramparted round with tyrant lies! But is it true? Am I what I seem to myself? Did I fail in my purpose, in my will? Did Italy herself belie me? Did she, did she I loved, she I worshipped, she the woman to whom I gave all, for whom I sacrificed all, did she, too, forsake me? Ah, no! you will tell me Italy is free. But I did not free her! She waits only to put on in Venice her tiara. And for that other one, that fair Austrian woman, that devil whom I serve and adore, that yellow-haired witch who brewed her incantations in my holiest raptures, -- she did not then play me foul, and falsely feign love to win me to disgrace? May all the woes in Heaven's hands fall on her!

God! what have I said? That I should live to ban her with a word! Did I say it? Oh, but it was vain! Woe for her? No, no! all blessings shower upon her, sunshine attend her, peace and gladness dwell about her! Traitress though she were, I must love her yet; I cannot unlove her; I would take her into my heart, and fold my arms about her. -- Oh, I pray you do not look upon me with that mocking smile! Pity me, rather! pity this wretched heart that longs to curse God and die! -- Nay, I want not your idle words. Can good destroy? Can love persecute? I was a worm that turned. What then? Why not have crushed me to annihilation? Oh, no, not that! He took me up and shook me before the world, clipped me, and let me fall. I derisive Deity, -- why, the words give each other the lie!

Stop! Your sad eyes look as if you would go away, but for this infinite pity in you. What makes you pity me? Because I am shorn of my strength? because of all my fair proportions there is nothing left unshrivelled? because my body -- such as it is -- is racked with hourly and perpetual pain? because I die? For none of these? Truly, your judgments are inscrutable. For what then? Because, -- yet, no, that cannot be, -- because I bear a stubborn heart? because I will not bend my soul as He has bent my body? Partly, -- but you are witless! What else? Because I toss off a shield and buckler, you say. Because I will not lean upon a tower of strength. Because I will not throw myself on the tide of divine love, and trust myself to its course. It was that divine love, then, that tower of strength, that shield and buckler, that made m this thing you see. Tarpeia was enough. Away with your generalities! Go, go, you slave of the past!

Yet no, -- you have not gone? You believe what you say, -- I know with those eyes you cannot deceive. Ah, but I trusted her eyes once! Yet it gives you rest; -- your sorrows are not like mine, -- there *is* no rest for me. I cannot go and gather that balm of Gilead, -- I have no legs. I have as good as none. This wheel-chair and that

dog of a turnkey are not the equipage for such a journey.
-- Ah, do not turn from me now! My railing is worse
than my cursing, you feel indeed. Well, stay with me at
least, and if it is twelve years since you shrived me at
first, perhaps you shall shrive me at last, -- for I doubt if I
am ever brought out to this sunshine again, if I do not
die in the prison-damps tonight, -- and you, with all
your change, are Father Anselmo, I think. -- Stay, I will
confess to you, confess this. Man! man! this infinite pity
of your soul for mine throws a light on my dark ways:
God's curse has fallen on me through man's curse, why
not God's love through man's love? Anselmo, though
you became priest, and I went to become hero, we were
children together; I was dear to you then; I am so still, it
seems. In your love let me find the love of that Heaven I
have defied. -- Stay, friend, yet another word. If man's
love can be so great, what can God's love be? That which
I said I said in desperation; in very truth, that peace
hangs like an unattainable city in the clouds before my
soul's vision, that love like a broad river flowing through
the lands, an atmosphere bathing the worlds, the subtile
essence and ether of space in which the farthest star
pursues its course, -- why, then, should it escape me, the
mote? Oh, when the world turned from me, I sought to
flee thither! I sighed for the rest there! Wretched, alone, I
have wept in the dark and in the light that I might go
and fling myself at the heavenly feet. But, do you see? sin
has broken down the bridge between God and me. Yet
why, then, is sin in the world, -- that scum that rises in
the creation and fermentation of good, -- why, but *as* a
bridge on which to re-seek those shores from which we

wander? Man, I do repent me, -- in loving you I find God. And you call that blasphemy! -- Nay, go, indeed, my friend! So humble, you are not the man for me. I can talk to the winds: they, at least, do not visit me too roughly.

These are thy tears, Anselmo? Thou a priest, yet a man? Still with me? Yet thou wilt have to bear with wayward moods, -- scorn now, quiet then. I am a tetchy man; I am an old man, too, though but just past thirty. -- So! I thank God for thee, dear friend!

Anselmo, look out on this scene below us here, as we sit on our lofty battlement. Not on the turrets of the loopholes, the grates and spikes, or all the fortified horror, -- but on the earth. It is fair earth, though not Italy; this is a mountain-fortress; here are all the lights and shadows that play over grand hill-countries, and yonder are fields of grain, where the winds and sunbeams play at storm, and a little hamlet's sheltered valley. Doubtless there are towers, besides, half hidden in the hills. It is Austria: slaves tread it, and tyrants drain it, it is true, -- but the wild, free gypsies troop now and then across it, and though no fiction of law supports a claim they would scorn to make, they use it so that you would swear they own it. Do you see how this iron reticulation of social rule and custom and force makes a scaffolding on which this tameless race build up their lives? I watch them often. Each country has its compensations. Anselmo, this first made me tremble in my petty defiance, -- I, an ephemera of May, defying the dominations of eternity! -- Not so, -- not too lowly; I also am, and each limitation of life is as well, a domination of eternity. But I saw that it was no purpose of God to have destroyed Italy; when men in weakness and wantonness suffered their liberties to be torn from them, suffered themselves to become enslaved, there was compensation in that their sons had chance for heroic growth; they might, in efforts for freedom, create virtues that, born to freedom, they would never have known. I, too, had my field; I lost it; my enemy was myself. But when I think of her -- Ay, there it is! Do not let me think of her! I become mad, when I think of her! -- At least, allow me this: God's ways are dark. Not that? Not even that? I needed what I have? If my ambitions, my passions, my will, had ruled, my soul would have remained null? Ah, friend, and is that so much the worse? It is the soul that aches! -- I am a man of the people, a man who acts, -- I *was*, I mean, -- not a man who thinks; and all your subtleties of word perchance entrap me. I am not wary when you come to logic. See! I surrender point after point. I shall be dead soon, you know; when this morning's sun shall have set, when the moon shall hold the night in fee, I shall depart, -- wing up and away; -- is it, that, my body already dead, my mind sickens and dies with it, bit after bit, and so I yield, and attest, that, without the agony of my life, death had failed to burst my soul's husk? Oh, for I was born of an earthy race, blood ran thick in our veins, we were sensuous and passionate, the breath and steam of pleasure stifled our brains, and our filmy eyes could not see heaven. Yes, yes, I needed it all; but, friend, it is pitiful.

I like to sit here in the sun. It is only a twelvemonth, of all my long years' imprisonment, that this has been allowed me. I like to sleep in it, like any wild creature, -- the lizard, a mere reptile, -- the bird, a hindered soul. To lie thus, weak as I am, but pillowed and warmed by the searching genial rays, seems such comfort, when I think of the bed I once had on the rack! This little slumber from which I wake revives me. I feared not to find you, and did not unclose my eyes at once. It was good in you to come, Anselmo; it must have been at risk of much.

You ask me to speak of my life since I went away on that morning of your command, -- to reconcile the hostile acts, to gather the scattered reports. Hear it all!

You know my wealth was equal to my demand. I used it; before six months were over, I was the life and soul of those who must needs be conspirators. They saw that I was earnest, that my sacrifices were real; they trusted me. Soon the movement had become general; all the smothered elements of national life were convulsed and throbbing under the crust of tyranny.

How proud and glad was I that morning after our victory! I saw great Italy, beautiful Italy, once more put on her diadem; I beheld the future prospect of one broad, free land, barriered by Alps and set impregnably in summer seas, storied seas, keys of the West and East. We embraced each other as brothers of this glorious nation, ancient Rome risen from trance; as we walked the streets, we sand; Milan was turbulent with gladness; no gala-day was ever half so bright; the very spires appeared to spring in the white radiance of their flames up a deeper heaven; the sun stayed at perpetual dawn for us. Walking along, jubilant and daring, at length we paused in a square where a fountain dashed up its column of sunshine, and laved our hands. By Heaven! We forgot independence, Italy, freedom; we were crazed with success and hope; it seemed that the stream was Austrian blood! Then, in the midst of all, I looked up, -- and on a balcony she stood. A fair woman, with hair like shredded light, her great blue eyes wide and full and of intense dye, her nostril distended with pride, and fear and hate of us, -- but on the full lips, ripe with crimson bloom, juicy and young and fresh, on those Love lay. The others wound forward, -- I with them, yet apart; and my eyes became fixed on hers. Then I lifted my cap with its tricolor. She did not return the courtesy, but stood as if spellbound, one hand threading back the straying hair, the lips a little parted; suddenly she turned to fly, that hand upraised to the casement's side, and still, as she looked back, the beautiful eyes on mine. My companions had preceded me; we were alone in the square; she wavered as she stood, then tore a rose from her bosom, kissed it deep into its heart, and tossed it to me.

"Let all its petals be joys!" I said, and she vanished.

Oh, friend, the leaves have fallen, the rose is dead! Look! I have kept it through all, -- sear leaf and withered spray!

That night we danced; and the Austrian girl was there. They told me she was exiled, and that she loved liberty; no one told me she was a spy. I saw her swim along the dance, the white satin of her raiment flashing perpetual interchange of lustrous and obscure, the warm air playing in the lace that fell like the spray of the fountain round her golden hair and over her pearly shoulder; grace swept in all her motions, beauty crowned her, she seemed the perfect pitch of womanhood.

Still she swims along the lazy line with indolent pleasure, still floats in dreamy waltz-circles perchance, still bends to the swaying tune as the hazel-branch bends to the hidden treasure, -- but as for me, my dancing days are over.

By-and-by it was I with whom she danced, whose hand she touched, on whom she leaned. I wondered if there were any man so blest; I listened to her breath, I watched her cheek, our eyes met, and I loved her. The music grew deeper, more impassioned; we stood and listened to it, -- for she danced then no more, -- our hearts beat time to it, the wind wandering at the casement played in its measure; we said no words, but now and then each sought the other's glance, and, convicted there, turned in sudden shame away. When I bade her good-night, which I might never have done but that the revel broke, a great curl of her hair blew across my lips. I was bold, -- I was heated, too, with this half-secret life of my heart, this warm blood that went leaping so riotously through my veins, and yet so silently, -- I took my dagger from my belt and severed the curl. See, friend! will you look at it? It is like the little gold snakes of the Campagna, is it not? each thread, so fine and fair, a separate ray of light: once it was part of her! See how it twists round my hand! Haste! haste! let me put it up, lest I go mad! -- Where was I?

I busied myself again in the work to be done; because of our victory we must not rest; once more all went forward. I saw the Austrian woman only from a window, or in a church, or as she walked in the gardens, for many days. Then the times grew hotter; I left the place, and lived with stern alarums; and thither she also came. I never sought what sent her. She was with the wounded, with the dying. Then the need of her was past, and she and all the others took their way. At length that also came to an end.

We were in Rome, -- and thither, some time previously, she had gone.

One night, our business for the day was over, our plans for the morrow laid, our messages received, our messengers despatched, and those who had been conspirators and now bade fair to be saviours were sleeping. Sleep seemed to fold the world; each bough and twig was silent in repose; the spectral moonlight itself slept as it bathed the air. I alone wandered and waked. With me there were too many cares for rest; work kept me on the alert; to court slumber at once was not easy after the nervous tension of duty. I was torn, too, with conflicting feelings: half my soul went one way in devotion to my country, half my soul swerved to the other as I thought of the Austrian woman. I grew tired of the streets and squares; something that should be fragrant and bowery attracted me. I mounted on the broken water-god of a dry bath and leaped a garden-wall.

No sooner was I there than I knew why I had come. This was her garden.

Heart of Heaven! how all things spoke of her! How the great white roses hung their doubly heavy heads and poured their perfume out to her! how the sprays shivered as I spoke the name she owned! how the nightingales ceased for a breath their warbling as she rustled down a fragrant path and met me! All her hair was swept back in one great mass and held by an ivory comb; a white cloak wrapped her white array; she was jewelless and stripped of lustre; she was like pearl, milky as a shell, white as the moonlight that followed in her wake.

"You breathed my name, -- I came," she said.

"Pardon!" I replied. "I heard the fountains dash and the nightingales sing, and I but came for rest under the spell."

"And have you found it?"

"I have found it."

We remained silent then, while floods of passion gathered and lay darkly still in our hearts. No, no! I know now that it was not so; yet I will tell it, tell it all, as I thought it then.

She did not stir; indeed, she had such capability of rest, that, had I not spoken, she would never have stirred, it may be. She knew that my glance was upon her; for herself, she looked at the broad lilies that grew at her feet, and listened to the melody that seemed to bubble from a thousand throats with interfluent sound upon the night. It was her repose that soothed me: moulded clay is not so calm, the marble rose of silence not half so beautifully folded to dreamful rest, so lovely and so still no garden-statue could have been; the cool, soft night infiltrated its tranquillity through all her being.

As we stood, the nightingales gave us capricious pause; one alone, distant and clear, fluted its faint piping like the phantom of the finished strain. Another sound broke the air and floated alone on this too delicious accompaniment: music, fine and far. Some other lover sang to her his serenade. The voice in its golden sonority rose and crept toward her with persuading sweetness, winding through all the alleys and hovering over the plots of greenery with a tranquil strength, as if such song

were but the natural spirit of the night, or as if the soul
of the broad calm and silence itself had taken voice.

"Thy beauty, like a star
Whose life is light,
Shines on me from afar,
And on the night.

"Each midnight blossom bends
With sweetest weight,
And to thy casement sends
Its fragrant freight.

"Each air that faintly curls
About thy nest
Its daring pinion furls
Within thy breast.

"The night is spread for thee,
The heavens are wide,
And the dark earth's mystery
Is magnified.

"For thee the garden waits,
The hours delay,
The fountains toss their jets

Of shimmering spray.

"Then leave thy dim delight
In dreams above,
Come forth, and crown the night
With her I love!"

She listened, but did not lift her head or suffer the change of a fold; then there came the tinkle of the strings that embalmed the tune, and the singer's steps grew soundless as he left the street. A new phantasm crept upon me. What right had any other man to sing to her his love-songs? Did she not live, was not her beauty created, her soul given, for me? Did not the very breath she drew belong to me? My voice, hoarse and husky, disturbed the stillness, my eyes flamed on her.

"Do you love that man who sang?" I murmured.

"Signor, I love you," she said.

Then we were silent as before, but she stood no longer alone and opposite. One passionate step, an outstretched arm, and her head on my bosom, my lips bent to hers.

All the nightingales burst forth in choral redundance of song, all the low winds woke and fainted again through the balmy boughs, all the great stars bent out of heaven to shed their sweet influences upon us.

It seemed to me that in that old palace-garden life began, my memory went out in confused joy. I held her, she was mine! mine, mine, in life and for eternity! Fool! it was I who was hers! Man, you are a priest, and must not love. I, too, was sworn a priest to my country. So we break oaths!

O moments of swift bliss, why are you torture to remember? Let me not think how the night slipped into dawn as we roamed, how pale gold filtered through the darkness and bleached the air, how bird after bird with distant chirrup and breaking tune announced the day. She left me, and as well it might be night. I wound a strange way home. I questioned if it were the dream of a fevered brain; I wondered, would she remember when next she saw me? None met with me that day; I forgot all. With the night I again waited in the garden. In vain I waited; she came no more. I waxed full of love's anger, I crushed the tendril and the vine, I wandered up and down the walks and cursed these thorns that tore my heart. As I went, an angle of the shrubbery allured; I turned, and lo! full radiance from open doors, and silvery sounds of sport. I leaned against the ilex, lost in shadow, and watched her as she stirred and floated there before me in the light. She seemed to carry with her an atmosphere of warmth and brilliance; all things were ordered as she moved; one throng melted before her, another followed. By-and-by she stood at the long casement to seek acquaintance with the night. Constantly I thought to meet her eye, and I would not reflect that she saw only dusk and vacancy. Then indignantly I stepped from the ilex and confronted her. A low, glad cry escapes her lips, she holds her arms toward me and would cross the sill, when a voice constrains her from within. It is he, the accursed Neapolitan.

"Signor," she says, "a vampire flitted past the dawn."

Dawn indeed was breaking. The man still stood there when she left him, and still looked out; his eyes lay on me, and irate and motionless I returned their gaze. One by one her guests departed; with a last threatening glance, he, too, withdrew. I plunged into the silent places again, and waited now, assured that she would come. The constellations paled, and still I was alone. Then I wandered restlessly again, and, winding through thickets of leaf-distilled perfume, I came where just above a balcony, and almost beyond reach from it, a light burned dimly in one narrow window. I did not ask myself why I did it, but in another moment I had clambered to the place, and standing there, I bent forward to my right, pulled away the tangle of ivy that filled half the niche, and was peering in.

"What is that?" said a voice I knew, with its silvery echo of the South, the accursed Neapolitan's.

"It is the owl that builds in the recess, and stirs the ivy," she replied.

"Haste!" said a third, -- "the day breaks."

She was sitting at a low table, writing; Pia, the old nurse, stood behind her chair; the oil was richly scented that she burned; the single light illumined only her, and covered with her shadow the low ceiling, -- a shadow that seemed to hang above her like a pall ready to fall from ghostly fingers and smother her in its folds; the others lounged about the room and waited on her pen, in gloom they, their faces gleaming from that dusk demoniacly. It was a concealed room, entered by secret ways, unknown to others than these.

When she had written, she sealed.

"There is no more to await. Adieu," she said.

"It is some transfer of property, some legal paper, some sale, some gift," I said to myself, as I watched them take it and depart. Then she was alone again. I saw her start up, pace the narrow spot, -- saw her stand and pull down the masses, so interspersed with golden light, that crowned her head, and look at them wonderingly as they overlay her fingers, -- then saw those fingers clasped across the eyes, and the lips part with a sigh that, prolonged and deepened, grew to be a groan, -- while all the time that shadow on the ceiling hovered and fluttered and grew still, till it seemed the cluster of

Eumenides waiting to pounce on its prey. In another pause I had taken the perilous step, had hung by the crumbling rock, the rending vine, had entered and was beside her. A cold horror iced her face; she warned me away with her trembling hands.

"What have you seen?" she said.

"You, O my love, in grief."

"And no more?"

"I have seen you give a letter to the Neapolitan, who departs to-morrow with the little Viennois, -- perhaps to your friends at home."

"And that is all?"

"That is all."

"I have no friends at home. To whom, then, could the letter be?"

"How should I divine?"

"It was for the Austrian Government! Now love me, if you dare!"

"And do you suppose I did not know it?"

"Then is your love for me but a shield and mask?"

As I gazed in reply, my steady eyes, the soul that kindled my smile, my open arms, all must have asseverated for me the truth of my devotion.

"Still?" she said. "Still? And you can keep your faith to me and to Italy?"

What was this doubt of me, this stain she would have cast upon my honor? That armor's polish was too intense to sustain it; it rolled off like a cloud from heaven. Italy's fortunes were *my* fortunes; it was impossible for me to betray them; this woman I would win to wed them. How long, how long my blood had felt this thing in her! how long my brain had rebelled! In a proud innocence, I stood with folded arms, and could afford to smile.

"Stay!" she said again, after our mute gaze, and laying her hand upon my arm. "You shall not love me in vain, you shall not trust me for nothing. Your cause is mine to-day. That is the last message I send to Vienna."

And then I believed her.

The light, slanting up, crept in and touched the brow of an ideal bust of Mithras which she had invested with her faintly-faded wreath of heliotropes; their fragrance falling through the place already made the atmosphere more rich than that of chest of almond-wood, -- this perfume that is like the soul of the earth itself exhaled to the amorous air. Behind an alabaster shrine she lighted a holy-taper, slowly to waste and pale in the spreading day. We went to the window, where among the ivy-nooks day's life was just astir with gaudy wings.

"All will be seeking you, and yet you cannot go," she said.

"Why can I not go?"

"It is broad morning."

"And what of that?"

"One thing. You shall not compromise yourself, going from the house of an Austrian woman and worse!"

She was too winningly imperious to fail. I delayed, and together we looked out on the rosy sky.

"Come down," she said at last, "and on an arbor-moss the sun shall drowse you, the flower-scents be your opiates, the birds your lullaby, and I your guard."

We went, and, wandering again through the garden-paths, she brushed the dew with her trailing festal garments, and plucked the great blue convolvuli to crown her forehead. Soon, on a plot of Roman violets, screened by tall trees and trellises, we breakfasted. One might have said that the cloth was laid above giant mushroom-stems, the service acorn-cups and calices of milky blooms; golden was the honey-comb we broke, manna was our bread; she caught the water in her hand from the fountain and pledged me, and swift as sunshine I bent forward and prevented the thirsty lips. Then she laid my head on her shoulder, with her cool finger-tips she stroked the temples and soothed the lids, they fell and closed on the vision bending above me, -- loveliness like painting, pallor that was waxen, yellow tresses wreathed with azure stars, eyes that caught the hue again and absorbed all Tyrian dyes.

The plash and bubble of waters swooned dreamily about my ears, and far off it seemed I heard the wild, sad songs of her native land, that now in tinkling tune, and now in long, slow rise and fall of mellow sound, swathed me with sweet satiety to dreamless rest.

The sun stole round and rose above the screen of trees at last and woke me. I was alone, the silent statues looked on me, the breath of the dark violets crushed by my weight rose in shrouding incense. I lifted myself and searched for her, and asked why I must needs believe each hour of joy a dream, -- then went and cooled my brow in the lucent basin at hand, and waited till she came, in changed raiment, and gliding toward me as the Spirit of Noon might have come. She led me in, well, refreshed, and in the cool north rooms of the palace the warm hours of the day slipped like beads from a leash. It scarcely seemed her fingers that touched the harp to tune, but as if some herald of sirocco, some faint, hot breeze, had brushed between the strings. It scarcely seemed her voice that talked to me, but something distant as the tone in a sad sea-shell. What I said I knew not; I was in a maze, bewildered with bliss; I only knew I loved her, I only felt my joy.

She told me many things: stories of her mountain-home, in distant view of the old fortress of Hellberg, -- this is the fortress of Hellberg, Anselmo, -- of her youth, her maidenhood, her life in Vienna, her lovers in Venice, her health, that had sent her finally there where we sat together.

"I thought it sad," she said at length, "when they exiled me, so to say, from Vienna and all my gay career there because Venice, with its water-breaths, might heal my attainted health, -- and sadder when the winter bade me leave night-tides and gondolas and repair to Rome. Now spring has come, and all the hills are blue with these deep violets, the very air is balm, the year is at flood, and life at what seems its height is perfected with you."

"But you love that land you left?" I replied, after a while, and lifting her face to meet my gaze.

"Love it? Oh, yes! You love your land as you love a person in whose veins and yours kindred blood runs, because it is hardly possible to do otherwise. The land gave me life, that is all; I never knew till lately that it was anything to be thankful for. It is not sufficiently a *country* to kindle enthusiasm; it has no national life, you know, -- is an automaton put through its motions by paid and cunning mechanists. I thought it right to obey orders and serve it. But now *you* are my country, -- I serve only you."

It was easy so to pass to my own hopes, to my own life, to my land, the land to which I had vowed the last drop of blood in my gift. Her eyes beamed upon me, smiles rippled over her face, she clasped me now and then and sealed my brow with kisses. Soon I left her side and strode from end to end of the long *salon*, speaking eagerly of the future that opened to Italy. I told her how the beautiful corpse lay waiting its resurrection, and how the Angel of Eternal Life hovered with spreading wings above, ready to sound his general trump. My pulses beat like trip-hammers, and as I passed a mirror I saw myself white with the excitement that fired me.

"You are wild with your joyous emotion," she said, coming forward and clinging round me. "Your eyes flame from depths of darkness. What, after all, is Italy to you, that your blood should boil in thinking of her wrongs? These people, for whom in your terrible magnanimity, I feel that you would sacrifice even me, to-morrow would turn and rend you!"

"No, no!" I answered. "All things but you! You, you, are before my country!"

The tears filled her large, serious eyes, her lips quivered in melancholy smile, as sunshine plays with shower over autumn woodlands. Was I not right? Right, though the universe declare me wrong! I would do it all again; if she loved me, she had authority to be first of all in my care; in love lie the highest duties of existence.

I had forgotten the subject on which we spoke; I was thinking only of her, her beauty, her tenderness, and the debt of deathless devotion that I owed her. It was otherwise in her thought; she had not dropped the old thread, but, looking up, resumed.

"It is, then, an idea that you serve?"

Brought back from my reverie, "Could I serve a more worthy master?" I asked.

"You do not particularly love your countrymen, nine-tenths of whom you have never seen? You do not particularly hate the hostile race, nine-tenths of whom you have never seen?"

"Abstractly, I hate them. Kindliness of heart prevents individual hatred, and without kindliness of heart in the first place there can be no pure patriotism."

"And for the other part. What do you care for these men who herd in the old tombs, raise a pittance of vetch, and live the life of brutes? what for the lazzaroni of Naples, for the brigands of Romagna, the murderers of the Appenine? Nay, nothing indeed. It is, then, for the land that you care, the mere face of the country, because it entombs myriad ancestors, because it is familiar in its every aspect, because it overflows with abundant beauty. But is the land less fair when foreign sway domineers it? do the blossoms cease to crowd the gorge, the mists to fill it with rolling color? is the sea less purple around you, the sky less blue above, the hills, the fields, the forests, less lavishly lovely?"

"Yes, the land is less fair," I said. "It is a fair slave. It loses beauty in the proportion of difference that exists between any two creatures, -- the one a slave of supple symmetry and perfect passivity, the other a daring woman who stands nearer heaven by all the height of her freedom. And for these people of whom you speak, first I care for them because they *are* my countrymen, -- and next, because the idea which I serve is a purpose to raise them into free and responsible agents."

"Each man does that for himself; no one can do it for another."

"But any one may remove the obstacles from another's way, scatter the scales from the eyes of the blind, strip the dead coral from the reef."

She took yellow honeysuckles from a vase of massed amethyst and began to weave them in her yellow hair, -- humming a tune, the while, that was full of the subtilest curves of sound. Soon she had finished, and finished the fresh thought as well.

"Do you know, my own," she said, "the men who begin as hierophants of an idea are apt to lose sight of the pure purpose, and to become the dogged, bigoted, inflexible, unreasoning adherents of a party? All leaders of liberal movements should beware how far they commit themselves to party-organizations. Only that man is free. It is easier to be a partisan then a patriot."

I laughed.

"Lady, you are like all women who talk politics, however capable they may be of acting them. You immediately beg the question. We are speaking of patriotism, not of partisanship."

"You it was who forsook the subject. You know nothing about it; you confess that it is with you merely a blind instinct; you cannot tell me even what patriotism is."

"Stay!" I replied. "All love is instinct in the germ. Can you define the yearnings that the mother feels toward her child, the tie that binds son to father? Then you can define the sentiment that attaches me to the land from whose breast I have drawn life. The love of country is more invisible, more imponderable, more inappreciable than the electricity that fills the air and flows with perpetual variation from pole to pole of the earth. It is as deep, as unsearchable, as ineffable as the power which sways me to you. It is the sublimation of other affection. A portion of you has always gone out into the material spot where you have been, a portion of that has entered you, your past life is entwined with river and shore. You become the country, and the country becomes a part of God. Those who love their country, love the vast abstraction, can almost afford not to love God. She is a beneficence, she is a shield, something for which to do and die, something for worship, ideal, grand; and though the sky is their only roof, the earth their only bed, affluent are they who have a land! Passion rooted deeply as the foundations of the hills: a man may adore one woman, but in adoring his land the aggregation of all men's love for all other women overwhelms him and accentuates to a fuller emotion. It is unselfish, impersonal, sheer sentiment clarified at its white heat from all interest and deceit, the noblest joy, the noblest sorrow. Bold should they be, and pure as the priests who bore the ark, that dare to call themselves patriots. And those, Lenore, who live to see their country's hopeless ruin, plunge into a sadness at heart that no other loss can equal, no remaining blessing mitigate, -- neither the devotion of a wife nor the perfection of a child. You have seen exiles from a lost land? Pride is dead in them, hope is dead, ambition is dead, joy is dead. Tell me, would you choose me to suffer the personal loss of love and you, a loss I could hide in my aching soul, or to bear those black marks of gall and melancholy which forever overshadow them in widest grief and gloom?"

She had sunk upon a seat, and was looking up at me with a pained unwavering glance, as if in my words she foresaw my fate.

"You are too intense!" she cried. "Your tones, your eyes, your gestures, make it an individual thing with you."

"And so it is!" I exclaimed. "I cannot sleep in peace, nor walk upon the ways, while these Austrian bayonets take my sunshine, these threatening approaching French banners hide the fair light of heaven!"

"Come," she said, rising. "Speak no more. I am tired of the burden of the ditty, dear; and it may do you such injury yet that already I hate it. Come out again into our garden with me. Dismiss these cares, these burning pains and rankling wounds. Be soothed by the cool evening air, taste the gorgeous quiet of sunset, gather peace with the dew."

So we went. I trusted her the more that she differed from me, that then she promised to love Italy only because *I* loved it. I told her my secret schemes, I took her advice on points of my own responsibility, I learned the joy of help and confidence in one whom you deem devotedly true. Finally we remained without speech, stood long heart to heart while the night fell around us like a curtain; her eyes deepened from their azure noon-splendor and took the violet glooms of the hour, a great planet rose and painted itself within them; again and again I printed my soul on her lips ere I left her.

At first, when I was sure that I was once more alone in the streets, I could not shake from myself the sense of her presence. I could not escape from my happiness, I was able to bring my thought to no other consideration. I reached home mechanically, slept an hour, performed the routine of bath and refreshment, and sought my former duties. But how changed seemed all the world to me! what air I breathed! in what light I worked! Still I felt the thrilling pressure of those kisses on my lips, still those dear embraces!

So days passed on. I worked faithfully for the purpose to which I was so utterly committed that let that be lost and I was lost! We were victorious; after the banner fell in Lombardy to soar again in Venice and sink, the Republic struggled to life; Rome rose once more on her seven hills, free and grand, child and mother of an idea, the idea of national unity, of independence and liberty from Tyrol to Sicily. My God! think of those dear people who for the first time said, "We have a country!"

Yet how could we have hoped then to continue? Such brief success dazzled us to the past. Piedmont had long since struck the key-note of Italy's fortunes. As Charles Albert forsook Milan and suffered Austria once more to mouth the betrayed land and drip its blood from her heavy jaws, till in a baptism of redder dye he absolved himself from the sin, -- so woe heaped on woe, all came to crisis, ruin, and loss, -- the Republic fell, Rome fell, the French entered.

Our names had become too famous, our heroic defence too familiar, for us to escape unknown: the Vascello had not been the only place where youth fought as the lioness fights for her whelps. Many of us died. Some fled. Others, and I among them, remained impenetrably concealed in the midst of our enemies. Weeks then dragged away, and months. New schemes chipped their shell. Again the central glory of the land might rise revealed to the nations. We never lost courage; after each downfall we rose like Antaeus with redoubled strength from contact with the beloved soil, for each fall plunged us farther into the masses of the people, into closer knowledge of them and kinder depths of their affection, and so, learning their capabilities and the warmth of their hearts and the strength of their endurance, we became convinced that freedom was yet to be theirs. Meanwhile, you know, our operations were shrouded in inscrutable secrecy; the French held Rome in frowning terror and subjection; the Pope trembled on his chair, and clutched it more franticly [sic] with his weak fingers: it was not even known that we, the leaders, were now in the city; all supposed us to be awaiting quietly the turn of events, in some other land. As if we ourselves were not events, and Italy did not hang on our motions! But, as I said, all this time we were at work; our emissaries gave us enough to do: we knew what spoil the robbers in the March had made, the decree issued in Vienna, the order of the day in Paris, the last word exchanged between the Cardinals, what whispers were sibilant in the Vatican; we mined deeper every day, and longed for the electric stroke which should kindle the spark and send princes and principalities shivered widely into atoms. But, friend, this was not to be. We knew one thing more, too: we knew at last that we also were watched, -- when men sang our songs in the echoing streets at night, and when each of us, and I, chief of all, renewed our ancient fame, and became the word in every one's mouth, so that old men blessed us in the way as we passed, wrapt, we had thought, in safe disguise, and crowds applauded. Thus again we changed our habits, our rendezvous, our quarters, and again we eluded suspicion.

There came breathing-space. I went to her to enjoy it, as I would have gone with some intoxicating blossom to share with her its perfume, -- with any band of wandering harpers, that together our ears might be delighted. I went as when, utterly weary, I had always gone and rested awhile with her I loved in the sweet old palace-garden: I had my ways, undreamed of by army or police or populace. There had I lingered, soothed at noon by the hum of the bee, at night by that spirit that scatters the dew, by the tranquillity and charm of the place, ever rested by her presence, the repose of her manner, the curve of her dropping eyelid, so that looking on her face alone gave me pleasant dreams.

Now, as I entered, she threw down her work, -- some handkerchief for her shoulders, perhaps, or yet a banner for those unrisen men of Rome, I said, -- a white silk square on which she had wrought a hand with a gleaming sickle, reversed by tall wheat whose barbed grains bent full and ripe to the reaper, and round the margin, half-pictured, wound the wild hedge-roses of Paestum. She threw it down and came toward me in haste, and drew me through an inner apartment.

"He has returned, they say," she said presently, -- mentioning the Neapolitan, -- "and it would be unfortunate, if you met."

"Unfortunate for *him*, if we met here!"

"How fearless! Yet he is subtler than the snake in Eden. I fear him as I detest him."

"Why fear him?"

"That I cannot tell. Some secret sign, some unspeakable intuition, assures me of injury through him."

"Dearest, put it by. The strength of all these surrounding leagues with their swarm does not flow through his wrist, as it does through mine. He is more powerless than the mote in the air."

"You are so confident!" she said.

"How can I be anything else than confident? The very signs in the sky speak for us, and half the priests are ours, and the land itself is an oath. Look out, Lenore! Look down on these purple fields that so sweetly are taking nightfall; look on these rills that braid the landscape and sing toward the sea; see yonder the row of columns that have watched above the ruins of their temple for centuries, to wait this hour; behold the heaven, that, lucid as one dome of amethyst, darkens over us and blooms in star on star; -- was ever such beauty? Ah, take this wandering wind, -- was ever such sweetness? And since every inch of earth is historic, -- since here rose glory to fill the world with wide renown, -- since here the heroes walked, the gods came down, -- since Oreads haunt the hill, and Nereids seek the shore" --

"Whereabout do Nereids seek the shore?" she archly asked.

"Why, if you must have data," I answered, laughing, "let us say Naples."

"What is that you have to say of Naples?" demanded a voice in the doorway, -- and turning, I confronted the Neapolitan.

She had started back at the abrupt apparition, and before she could recover, stung by rage and surprise I had replied, --

"What have I to say of Naples? That its tyrant walks in blood to his knees!"

A man, I, with my hot furies, to be intrusted with the commonwealth!

"I will trouble you to repeat that sentence at some day," he said.

"Here and now, if you will!" I uttered, my hand on my hilt.

"Thanks. Not here and now. It will answer, if you remember it *then*. -- I hope I see Her Highness well. Pardon this little *brusquerie*, I pray. The southern air is kind to loveliness: I regret to bring with me Her Highness's recall."

She replied in the same courteous air, inquired concerning her acquaintance, and ordered lights, -- took the letter he brought, and held it, still sealed, in the taper's flame till it fell in ashes.

"Signor," she said, lifting the white atoms of dust and sifting them through her fingers, "you may carry back these as my reply."

"Nay, I do not return," he answered. "And, Signorina, many things are pardoned to one in -- your condition. Recover your senses, and you will find this so among others."

Then, as coolly as if nothing had happened, he spoke of the affairs of the day, the tendency of measures, the feeling of the people, and finally rose, kissed her hand, and departed. He was joined without by the little Viennois, and the accursed couple sauntered down the street together. I should have gone then, -- the place was no longer safe for me, -- but something, the old spell, yet detained me.

Lenore did not speak, but threw open all the windows and doors that were closed.

"Let us be purified of his presence, at least!" she cried, when this was done.

"And you have ceased to fear this man whom you have dared so offend?" I asked.

"He is not offended," said Lenore. "Austria is not Naples. He will not transmit my reply till he is utterly past hope."

"Hope of what?"

"Of my hand."

"Lenore! Then put him beyond hope now! Become my wife!"

"Ah, -- if it were less unwise" --

"If you loved me, Lenore, you would not think of that."

"And you doubt it? Why should I, then, say again that I love you, -- I love you?"

Ah, friend, how can I repeat those words? Never have I given her endearments again to the air: sacred were they then, sacred now, however false. Ah, passionate words! oh, sweet *issimos*! tender intonations! how deeply, how deeply ye lie in my soul! Let me repeat but one sentence: it was the key to my destiny.

"Yes, yes," she said, rising from my arms, "already I do you injury. You think oftener of me than of Italy."

It was true. I sprang to my feet and began pacing the floor, as I sought to recall any instance in which I had done less than I might for my country. The cool evening-breeze, and the bell-notes sinking through the air from distant old campaniles, soothed my tumult, and, turning, I said, --

"My devotion to you sanctifies my devotion to her. And not only for her own sake do I work, but that you, you, Lenore, may have a land where no one is your master, and where your soul may develop and become perfect."

"And those who have not such object, why do they work?"

Then first I felt that I had fallen from the heights where my companions stood. This ardent patriotism of mine was sullied, a stain of selfishness rose and blotted out my glory, others should wear the conquering crowns of this grand civic game. Oh, friend! that was sad enough, but it was inevitable. Here is where the crime came in, -- that, knowing this, I still continued as their leader, suffered them to call me Master and Saviour, and walked upon the palms they spread.

Lenore mistook my silence.

"You cannot tell me why they work?" she said. "From habit, from fear, because committed? It cannot be, then, that they are in earnest, that they are sincere, that they care a rush for this cause so holy to you. They have entered into it, as all this common people do, for the love of a new excitement, for the pleasurable mystery of conspiracy, for the self-importance and gratulation. They will scatter at the signal of danger, like mischievous boys when a gendarme comes round the corner. They will betray you at the lifting of an Austrian finger. Leave them!"

This was too much to hear in silence, -- to hear of these faithful comrades, who had endured everything, and were yet to overcome because they possessed their souls in patience, each of whom stood higher before God than I in unspotted public purity, and whose praise and love led me constantly to larger effort. At least I would make them the reparation of vindication.

"You mistrust them?" I exclaimed. "They whose souls have been tried in the furnace, who have the temper of fine steel, pliant as gold, but incorruptible as adamant, -- heroes and saints, they stand so low in your favor? Come, then, come with me now, -- for the bells have struck the hour, and shadows clothe the earth, -- come to their conclave where discovery is death, and judge if they be idle prattlers, or men who carry their lives in their hands!"

Fool! Fool! Fool! Every sound in the air cries out that word to me: the bee that wings across the tower hums it in my ear; the booming alarm-bell rings it forth; my heart, my failing heart, beats it while I speak. I would have carried a snake to the sacred ibis-nest, and thenceforth hope was hollow as an egg-shell!

She ran from the room, but, pausing in the door-way, exclaimed, --

"Remember, if you take me there, that I am no Roman patriot, -- I! I, who am of the House of Austria, that House that wears the crown of the Caesars, those Caesars who swayed the very imperial sceptre, who trailed the very imperial purple of old Rome! I endure the cause because it is yours. I beseech you to be faithful to it; because I should despise you, if for any woman you swerved from an object that had previously been with you holier than heaven!"

I stood there leaning from the lofty window and looking down over the wide, solitary fields. Recollections crowded upon me, hopes rose before me. One day, that yet lives in my heart, Anselmo, sprang up afresh, a day forever domed in memory. Fair rose the sun that day, and I walked on the nation's errands through the streets of a distant town, -- a hoar and antique place, that sheltered me safely, so slight guard was it thought to need by our oppressors. It pleased that reverend arch-hypocrite to take at this hour his airing. Late events had given the people courage. It was a market-day, peasants from the country obstructed the ancient streets, the citizens were all abroad. Not few were the maledictions muttered over a column of French infantry that wound along as it returned to Rome from some movement of subjection, not low the curses showered on an officer who escorted ladies upon their drive. As I went, I considered what a day it would have been for *emeute*, and what mortal injury *emeute* would have done our cause. Italy, we said, like fools, but honest fools, must not be redeemed with blood. As if there were ever any sacred pact, any new order of things, that was not first sealed by blood! Therefore, when I, alone perhaps of all the throng, saw one man -- a man in whose soul I knew the iron rankled -- stealing behind the crowd, behind the monuments, and, as the coach of His Excellency rolled luxuriously along, levelling a glittering barrel, -- it was but an instant's work to seize the advancing creatures, to hold them rearing, -- and then a deadly flash, -- while the ball whistled past me, grazed my hand, and pierced the leader's heart. In a twinkling the dead horse was cut away, and His Excellency, cowering in the bottom of the coach, galloped home more swiftly than the wind, without a word. But the populace appreciated the action, took it up with *vivas* long and loud, that rang after me when I had slipped away, and before nightfall had echoed in all ears through leagues of country round. I went that night to the theatre. The house was filled, and, as we entered, a murmur went about, and then cries broke forth, -- the multitude rose with cheers and bravos, calling my name, intoxicated with enthusiasm, and dazzled, not by a daring feat, but by the spirit that prompted it. Women tore off their jewels to twist them into a sling for my injured hand; men rose and made me a conqueror's ovation; the orchestra played the old Etrurian hymns of freedom; I was attended home with a more than Roman triumph of torch and song, stately men and beautiful women. But chameleons change their tint in the sunshine, and why should men always march under one color? Friend, not six months later there came another day, when triumph was shame, -- plaudits, curses, -- joyous tumult, scorching silence. Oh! -- -- - But I shall come to that in time. Now let me hasten; the hours are less tardy than I, and they bring with them my last.

Thought of this day -- sole pageant defiling through memory -- was startled again by the far, sweet sound of a bell, some bell ringing twilight out and evening in across the wide Campagna. I wondered what delayed Lenore. Did it take so long to toss off the cloudy back-falling veil, to wrap in any long cloak her gown of white damask and all the sheen of her milky pearl-clusters and fiery rubies? I thought with exultation then of what she was so soon to see, -- of the route through sunken ruins, down wells forsaken of their pristine sources and hidden by masses of moss, winding with the faint light in our hands through the awful ways and avenues of the catacombs. The scene grew real to me, as I mused. Alone, what should I fear? These silent hosts encamped around would but have cheered their child. But with her, every murmur becomes a portent of danger, every current of air gives me fresh tremors; as we pass casual openings into the sky, the vault of air, the glint of stars, shall seem a malignant face; I fancy to hear impossible footsteps behind us, some bone that crumbling falls from its shelf makes my heart beat high, her dear hand trembles in my hold, and, full of a new and superstitious awe, I half fear this ancient population of the graves will rise and surround us with phantom array. Now and then, a cold, lonely wind, blowing from no one knows where, rises and careers past us, piercing to the marrow. I think, too, of that underground space, half choked with rubbish, into which we are to emerge at last, once the hall of some old Roman revel. I see the troubled flashes flung from the flaring torch over our assembly. Alert and startled, I see Lenore listen to the names as if they summoned the wraiths and not the bodies of men whom she had supposed to be lost in the pampas of Paraguay, dead in the Papal prisons, sheltered in English homes, or tossing far away on the long voyages of the Pacific seas. I see myself at length taking the torch from its niche and restoring it, as a hundred times before, to

Pietro da Valambo, while it glitters on some strange object looking in at the vine-clad opening above with its breaths of air, serpent or hare, or the large face and slow eyes of a browsing buffalo. And as I think, lo! an echo in the house, a dull tramp in the hall, a stealthy tread in the room, a heavy hand upon my shoulder, -- I was arrested for high treason.

Do not think I surrendered then. Without a struggle I would be the prize of Pope nor King nor Kaiser! I shook the minions' grasp from my shoulder, I flashed my sword in their eyes; and not till the crescent of weapons encircled me in one blinding gleam, vain grew defence, vain honor, vain bravery. Of what use was my soul to me thenceforth? I became but carrion prey. I fell, and the world fell from me.

Sensation, emotion, awoke from their swooning lapse only in the light of day, the next or another, I knew not which. I was lifted from some conveyance, I saw blue reaches of curving bay and the great purifying priest of flame, and knew I was in the city guarded by its pillar of cloud by day, of fire by night. I had reason to know it, when, yet unfed, unrested, faint, smirched and smeared with blood and travel, loaded with chains, I was brought to a tribunal where sat the sleek and subtle tyrant of Naples.

"Signor," said a bland voice from the king's side, -- and looking in its direction, I encountered the Neapolitan, -- "Signor, I lately said that at some day I would trouble you to repeat a brilliant sentence addressed to me. The day has arrived. I scarcely dared dream it would be so soon. Shall we listen?"

I was silent: not that I feared to say it; they could but finish their play.

Then I saw the beautifully cut lips of my judge part, that the voice might slide forth, and, taking a comfit, he uttered, with unchanging tint and sweetest tone, the three words, "Apply the question."

Why should I endure that for a whim? Who courts torment? Already they drew near with the cunning instruments. Let me say it, and what then? Nothing worse than torture. Let me *not* say it, and certainly torture. Oh, I was weaker than a child! my body ruled my spirit with its exhaustion and pain. Yet there was a certain satisfaction in flinging the words in their faces. I waved back with my remaining arm the slaves who approached.

"You should allow a weary man the time to collect his thoughts," I said, and then turned to my persecutors. "I have spoken with you many times, Signor," I replied to the Neapolitan, "yet of all our words I can remember none but these, that you could care to hear with this auditory. I said, -- that the tyrant of Naples walks in blood to his knees!"

The Neapolitan smiled. The king rose.

"Well said!" he murmured, in his silvery tones. "One that knows so much must know more. Exhaust his knowledge, I pray. Do not spare your courtesies; remember he is my guest. I leave him in your hands."

He fixed me with his eye, -- that darkly-glazed eye, devoid of life, of love, of joy, as if he were the thing of another element, -- then bowed and passed away.

"The urbanity of His Majesty is too well known to suppose it possible that he should prove you a liar," said the Neapolitan.

Truly, I was left in their hands! Shall I tell you of the charities I found there? Not I, friend! it would wring your heart as dry of tears as mine was wrung of groans. At last I was alone, it seemed, -- on a wet stone floor, sweat pouring from every muscle, each fibre quivering; I was distorted and unjointed, I only hoped I was dying. But no, that was too good for me. Anselmo, how can I but be full of scoffs, when I remember those hours, those ages? The cold dampness of the place crept into my bones; I became swollen and teeming with intimate pain. But that was light, my body might have ached till the throbs stiffened into death-spasms, and yet the suffering had been nought, compared with that loathing and disgust in my soul. It had seemed that I was alone, I said. Alone as the corpse in unshrouded grave! I was in a charnel-house. Men who were sinless as you hung dead upon the wall, hung dying there. Darkness covered all things at a distance, sighs crept up from far corners, chains clanked, or imprecations or prayers uttered themselves, -- bodiless voices in the night. I did not know what untold horror there might yet be hid. I heard the drip of water from the black vaults; I heart the short, fierce pants and deadly groans. Oh, worst infliction of Hell's armory it is to see another suffer! Why was it allowed, Anselmo? Did it come in the long train of a broken law? was it one of the dark places of Providence? or was it indeed the vile compost to mature some beautiful germ? Ah, then, is it possible that Heaven looks on us so in the mass?

But for me, after a while I lay torpid, and then perchance I slept, for finally I opened my eyes and found the white strong light; I lay on a bed, and a surgeon handled me. Too elastic was I to be long crushed, once the weight removed. Soon I breathed fresh air; and save that my frame had become in its distortion hideous, I was the same as before.

Then, indeed, began my torture, -- torture to which this had been idle jest. I was taken once more to the room of tribunal. Beside the Neapolitan a woman sat veiled and shrouded in masses of sable drapery. "A queen?" I thought, "or a slave?" But I had no further room for fancy; the same interrogatories as before were given me to answer, and then I felt why I had been nursed back to life. In the months that had elapsed, I could not know if Italy were saved or lost, if Naples tottered or remained impregnable. I stood only on my personal basis of right or wrong. I refused to open my lips. They wheeled forward a low bed that I knew well. Oh, the slow starting of the socket! Oh, the long wrench of tendon and nerve! A bed of steel and cords, rollers and levers, bound me there, and bent to their creaking toil. I was strong to endure; I had set my teeth and sworn myself to silence; no woman should hear me moan. Even in this misery I saw that she who sat there, shaking, fell.

The tyrant was lily-livered; seldom he witnessed what others died under; he intended nothing further then; -- many men who faint at sight of blood can probe a soul to its utmost gasp. Now he motioned, and they paused. Then others lifted the woman and held her beside him, yet a little in advance.

"Keep your silence," said he, in a voice unrecognizable, and as if a wild beast, half-glutted, should speak, "and I keep her! She is in my power. Mine, and you know what that means. Mine," and he bent toward me, " *body -- and -- soul.* To use, to blast, to destroy, to tear piecemeal, -- as I will do, so help me God! unless you meet my condition." And extending his hand, he drew aside the black veil, and my eye lay on the face of Lenore, thin and white as the familiar faces of corpses, and utterly insensible in swoon.

Ah, that mortal horror stops my pulse! Was I wrong? Why not have borne that, too? Had she loved me, she had chosen it, chosen it rather. And death would have made all right! -- God! why not have seized some poignard lying there? why not have sprung upon her, have slain her? Then silence had been simply secure. Then I could have smiled in their frustrated faces, one keen, deep smile, and died. I was dissolved in pain, writhed with prolonged strokes that thrilled me from head to foot, pierced as with acute stabs, my heart seemed to forge thunderbolts to break upon my brain, -- but this agony had been spared me. They unbound me, fed me with some stimulating cordial, gave me cold air, and I rose on my elbow a little.

"Swear!" I said, hoarsely. "But you do not keep oaths. God help you? Never! There must be a Hell to help you! Imprecate this, then, on yourself. May you in your smooth white body know the torture I have known, be racked till each bone in your skin changes place, hang festering in chains from the wall of a living grave, make fellowship with putridity, and lie in the pitiless dark to see all the dead who died under your hand rise, rise and accuse you before God! And may your little son know the deeds you have done, live the life those deeds merit, and die the death that *I* shall die, -- if you do not keep your word!"

"What word?" he said.

"Promise, if I reveal all, and my revelations shall be true and thorough therefore, -- promise that you will leave her in safe security and freedom to-day, untouched, unscathed, unharmed, and that so ever shall she remain. And false to this oath, may no priest shrive you, no land own you, God blight you and curse you and wither you from the face of the earth!"

And taking a crucifix, he swore the oath.

Then they busied themselves about Lenore, revived her, soothed her, gave her of the same cordial to drink, and placed her once more in her dais-seat. Her veil was thrown back, her wide blue eyes fixed on me in intense strain, her face and lips still blanched more bitterly beneath that hue, her features sharp as chisel-graven death. Ah, God! must I endure that too? Was she to hear me, -- she, not knowing why, never knowing why, -- she in whom that look of aching passion and pity was to die out and freeze and fade in one of utter scorn?

They brought me some strange draught, as if one swallowed fire. The blood coursed richly through my shrunken veins; I felt filled with a different life. I arose and left that bed of torture, but came back to it as to my rest.

And lying there, I betrayed Italy.

Root and branch and spray and leaf, I uprooted all my memories; I forgot no name, I lost no fact; I was eagerer than they; I modified nothing, I abbreviated nothing; the past, the future, what had been, was to be, plan and scheme and supreme purpose, I never faltered, I told the whole!

I did not look at her, I kept my eyes on the tyrant; I wished I might have the evil eye, -- but that gift was for him, the Neapolitan. Yet at length I heard a low moan trailing toward me; I turned and saw her face, as I saw it last, Anselmo, -- stonily quiet, frozen from indignant pain to icy apathy, and the words she would have said had hissed inarticulately through her ashen lips. Then they brought me the confession, and, as I could, I signed it.

"Madame," said the tyrant, "your knowledge is coextensive with his. Does all this agree?"

"Sire, it does agree," she answered, and they led her out.

"I have no authority over you," said the tyrant then to me. "You might go freely now, but that, precious as Homer, seven cities claim you, Signor! My prisons also will now be full of rarer game. But as a crime of your commission places you within Austrian jurisdiction, I shall take pleasure in presenting you to my cousin and surrendering you to his mercy," and he withdrew.

"You may not be aware," said the courteous Neapolitan, "that on the night of your arrest your frantic sword-slashes had serious result. My friend the little Viennois fell at your hands."

"God be praised," I answered, "that I do not die without one good work!"

"Well said! And worthy of a traitor both to his ancient blood and to his cause, -- the betrayer of comrade and friend!"

I do not know what look was in my eye, or whether, with the savage ferocity taught me but now, I was about to leap and throttle him, and suck the life-blood from his veins. But suddenly he laughed, a feigned merriment, twirled his moustache, opened a door, looked back, uttering this one sentence: --

"You have simply corroborated her statement: you are not even the first in at the death: Lenore told all this more swiftly, with a better grace, and a something less sardonic mute-comment," -- closed the door and was gone. The breath of the bottomless pit had blown in my face.

They gave themselves time to swoop down and pounce on every man whose name I had given, and others; they prevented future trouble, they made terrible examples, they sated themselves with vengeance. But their feet were shod with velvet, -- history will never record it; to the world I and those nameless ones pass as mere idle agitators, bubbles that blew out to sea, -- but at my mention kings in their closet remember how their thrones trembled! Then they looked about them for one last morsel, and I was led to Rome.

O stormy days that I have to remember! O wild mornings of the cannonade, and of the sally! One noon blots ye all out in sullen darkness!

It was a gala-day, the day when I passed through; all the populace were out, my signed confession placarded the corners, Pasquin harvested my sins, Church and State made holiday. Cries of derision awaited me, ribald laughter, taunting jests, hisses and groans, gleaming stilettos, shining barrels, eyes of rage. But when I reached them, all was silence; silence closed up the ranks behind me. The shouting crowds grew noiseless, breathless. They each received the terrible impress of him who passed, -- his brow was branded as by doom; he went out Cain, and carried with him the curse of a ruined people. I gazed right and left, -- on these men who had once hailed me, followed me, worshipped me; their hate melted as they met my eye; slowly a cloud of terror and pity gathered and hung above the city. I did not repent; I would have done it again: not for a universe of Italies would I have resigned *her* to that fate. But, O friend, this forgiveness of theirs was unmerciful! For hate they had cause; for this none: they knew nothing of my reason, they only knew that I had betrayed them. Each man had despised me; he thought that to save my limbs like a young god's, to keep my face that had been splendid in youth's beauty, to spare that shape of antique symmetry and grace, to win ease and rest and wealth and happiness, perhaps, I had done this. Each man, as I met his gaze, shrunken, dismembered, deformed, dishonored, held his breath, shook with indefinable fear, felt the neighborhood of agony and despair, and forgave, forgave: -- oh! to live to be forgiven! But the women, -- the women, Anselmo, were not so cruel. There were torrents of streamers, but all were black, pouring from window and roof, -- there were sunny heads, and dark, fair faces, rosy cheeks, snowy shoulders, clustered in door and arch like bunches of poison-flowers, -- and of all shrill sounds of hate, Anselmo, that can pierce and part red lips, the fiercest, shrillest, fell on me; and at last, from one lofty balcony, where erst I had seen her leaning forth in sunset to catch the evening winds, the evening bells, crowned, too, by the evening star, one woman, now centred in merciless mid-noon, leaned, leaned and gazed down as into her grave: it was Lenore. It had been late spring when last I passed that way; all the hot, pestilential summer I had lain in the dungeons of Naples; now it was autumn, and the town was full. Full, but I saw no one; blank became the spaces on which I gazed; my gyves vanished, my guards; my brain swam through dazzling rings of light, and I fell forward in the cart and hung by my chains among the hoofs of the trampling horses who dragged me. On that day I had taken my last step; I never set foot on the round earth again. But, with all, I smiled through my groans; for the shining, solid hoofs that did their work on me did their work as well on the man who walked by my side, -- dashed dead the accursed Neapolitan.

They were not the surgeons of Naples who essayed to galvanize volition through my paralyzed limbs, but those who knew the utmost resources of their art. And so I lived, -- lived, too, by reason of my inextinguishable vitality, by reason of this spark that will not quench, -- and so I came to Hellberg. It would have been mockery to give this shapeless hulk to sentence, and then to headsman or hangman; perhaps, too, her haughty name had been involved; and so I was never brought to trial, and so I am at Hellberg.

And I have never set foot on the ground again. But, oh, to touch it for a moment, to sit anywhere on the summer mould, to pull down the sun-quivering, sun-steeped branches about me, to scent the fresh grass as it springs to the light! Oh, but to touch the sweet, kind earth, the warm earth, silent with ineffable tenderness and soothing, to feel it under my hand, to lay my cheek there for a moment, while it drew away pain and weariness with its absorbing, purifying power! Oh, but to lie once more where the blossoms grow! Soon, soon, they will grow above me! Soon the kind mother will cover me!

What had happened in the outer world I knew not till you came. I fancied Lenore returned, breathing Austrian air, and living under the same horizon that girds me in. Sometimes I have seen a distant cavalcade skimming over the vale, as once we careered over the Campagna, when she handled her steed as another woman handles her needle, and the sweet wind fanned peach-tints to her cheeks and drew out unravelled braids of gold in lingering caress. She could have come to me, had she pleased, then: this old chief who rules the place was her father's friend and hers. -- But look! but see! Who is it comes now, -- sweeps round the donjon flank? Lean over the embrasure, and learn! Ah, man, are my eyes so old, my memories so treacherous, that I do not know day from night? They have gone on, -- or did they enter, think you? Or yet, there is to be carousal, perhaps, in the halls beyond and below, and she comes to join the gay feast; she will drink healths in red wine, will listen to flattering dalliance with pleased eyes, will utter light laughs through the lips that once glowed to my kisses, and will forget that the same roof which shelters the revellers shelters also her lover dying in moans? Careless - - -- - Best so! best so! What cavalier whispered in her ear as she passed? Have years tarnished her beauty? Ah, God! this wind, that maddens me now, a moment since touched her!

Anselmo, I will go in. This vault of heaven with its spotless blue, this wide land that laughs in festive summer, these winds that lift my hair and come heavy with odors, -- these do not fit with me, I burlesque the fair face of creation. O invisible airs, that softly sport round the castle-towers, why do you not woo my soul forth and bear it and lose it in the flawless cope of sky?

Nay, why, any more than Ajax, should I die in the dark? Never again will I enter the cell, never again! The wide universe shall receive my breath. Lower the back of my chair, pull away the cushions, wrap my cloak round me, Anselmo. There! I will lie, and wait, and look up. Give me ghostly counsel, my friend, console me. You are not too weary with this long tale? Tell me I needed all the tears I have shed to quench the fiery defiance, the independence of heaven and tumult of earth in my being. If you could tell me that she had not been false, that she never feigned her passion to decoy, that, Austrian though she were -- -- - Ah, but I had evidence! I had evidence! his words, that ate out my life like gangrene and rust. -- Speak slower, Anselmo, slower. Can it be that I sinned most, when I held his words before hers, -- his black damning falsehoods? -- Mother of God! do you know what you say?

Tell me, then, that I am a fool, -- that not through other loss than the loss of faith did the curse fall on me! Tell me, then, that these dark ways lead me out on a height! Needful the shadow and the groping. He anointed my eyes with the clay beneath his feet, -- I was blind, but now I see God!

Repeat, Anselmo, repeat that she was true, though the knowledge blast me with self-consuming pangs. But, true or false, one thing she promised me: though other spheres, though other lives had come between us, she would be with me in my dying hour. Soon the bell will toll that hour, and toll my knell!

What is this, Anselmo, -- this face that hangs between me and heaven, -- this pitying, sorrowing countenance? -- Ave Maria! -- Never! Never! Still of the earth, this melting mouth, these violet eyes, this brow of snow, this fragrant bosom pillowing my head! Mirage of fainting fancy, -- out, beautiful thing, away! Do not torment me with such a despairing lie! do not cheat me into death! let me at least look on the unobstructed sky, as I sink lower and lower to my eternal rest!

Still there? Still there? Still bending above me, smiling and weeping, sweet April face? Oh, were they truly thy lips that lay on mine, then, that stamped them with life's impress, that woke me? Are they truly thy fingers that pressed my throbless temples? These arms that are wound about me, are thine? Thy heart beats for me, thy tears flow, thy perfect womanhood does not recoil in horror? Lenore! Lenore! is it thou?

Nay, nay, Sweet, ask me no question; I have wronged thee; he shall tell thee how. Yet best thou shouldst never hear it. Sin to thee greater than all treachery had been. Forgive, forgive! I go, -- in meeting, leave thee; but be glad for me, -- whether I sleep or whether I wake, know that a great curse will have fallen from me. Swathe my memory in thy love. Kiss me again, child! Rock me a little; stoop lower, and croon those old mountain-songs that once you sang when the sunshine soaked the sward and your hair was crowned with blue morning-glories.

Ah, your song drowns in tears! Yet you do not wish me to live, Lenore? O love, I can do nothing but die!

The sunlight fades from the hills, the air wavers and glimmers, and day is dim. Thy face is mistier than a vision of angels. There are faint, strange voices in my ear, swift rustlings, far harmonies; -- has sense become so attenuated that I hear the blood in my failing pulses? Lenore, love, lower. Thy lips to mine, and breathe my life away. Twice would I die to save thee!

-- Anselmo! man! where art thou? Come back ere I fall, -- strength flares up like a dying flame. *Never tell her why I betrayed Italy!*

-- Closer, dear love, closer! What old murmurs do I hear?

"The night is spread for thee,
The heavens are wide,
And the dark earth's mystery" --

So, -- in thy arms, -- from thee to God! O love, forever -- kiss -- forgive! -- Life me, that I confront eternity and Christ!

CIRCUMSTANCE

She had remained, during all that day, with a sick neighbor,--those eastern wilds of Maine in that epoch frequently making neighbors and miles synonymous,-- and so busy had she been with care and sympathy that she did not at first observe the approaching night. But finally the level rays, reddening the snow, threw their gleam upon the wall, and, hastily donning cloak and hood, she bade her friends farewell and sallied forth on her return. Home lay some three miles distant, across a copse, a meadow, and a piece of woods,--the woods being a fringe on the skirts of the great forests that stretch far away into the North. That home was one of a dozen log-houses lying a few furlongs apart from each other, with their half-cleared demesnes separating them at the rear from a wilderness untrodden save by stealthy native or deadly panther tribes.

She was in a nowise exalted frame of spirit,--on the contrary, rather depressed by the pain she had witnessed and the fatigue she had endured; but in certain temperaments such a condition throws open the mental pores, so to speak, and renders one receptive of every influence. Through the little copse she walked slowly, with her cloak folded about her, lingering to imbibe the sense of shelter, the sunset filtered in purple through the mist of woven spray and twig, the companionship of growth not sufficiently dense to band against her, the sweet home-feeling of a young and tender wintry wood.

It was therefore just on the edge of the evening that she emerged from the place and began to cross the meadow-land. At one hand lay the forest to which her path wound; at the other the evening star hung over a tide of failing orange that slowly slipped down the earth's broad side to sadden other hemispheres with sweet regret. Walking rapidly now, and with her eyes wide-open, she distinctly saw in the air before her what was not there a moment ago, a winding-sheet,--cold, white, and ghastly, waved by the likeness of four wan hands,--that rose with a long inflation, and fell in rigid folds, while a voice, shaping itself from the hollowness above, spectral and melancholy, sighed,-- "The Lord have mercy on the people! The Lord have mercy on the people!" Three times the sheet with its corpse-covering outline waved beneath the pale hands, and the voice, awful in its solemn and mysterious depth, sighed, "The Lord have mercy on the people!" Then all was gone, the place was clear again, the gray sky was obstructed by no deathly blot; she looked about her, shook her shoulders decidedly, and, pulling on her hood, went forward once more.

She might have been a little frightened by such an apparition, if she had led a life of less reality than frontier settlers are apt to lead; but dealing with hard fact does not engender a flimsy habit of mind, and this woman was too sincere and earnest in her character, and too happy in her situation, to be thrown by antagonism, merely, upon superstitious fancies and chimeras of the second-sight. She did not even believe herself subject to an hallucination, but smiled simply, a little vexed that her thought could have framed such a glamour from the day's occurrences, and not sorry to lift the bough of the warder of the woods and enter and disappear in their sombre path. If she had been imaginative, she would have hesitated at her first step into a region whose dangers were not visionary; but I suppose that the thought of a little child at home would conquer that propensity in the most habituated. So, biting a bit of spicy birch, she went along. Now and then she came to a gap where the trees had been partially felled, and here she found that the lingering twilight was explained by that peculiar and perhaps electric film which sometimes sheathes the sky in diffused light for many hours before a brilliant aurora. Suddenly, a swift shadow, like the fabulous flying-dragon, writhed through the air before her, and she felt herself instantly seized and borne aloft. It was that wild beast--the most savage and serpentine and subtle and fearless of our latitudes--known by hunters as the Indian Devil, and he held her in his clutches on the broad floor of a swinging fir-bough. His long sharp claws were caught in her clothing, he worried them sagaciously a little, then, finding that ineffectual to free them, he commenced licking her bare arm with his rasping tongue and pouring over her the wide streams of his hot, foetid breath. So quick had this flashing action been that the woman had had no time for alarm; moreover, she was not of the screaming kind: but now, as she felt him endeavoring to disentangle his claws, and the horrid sense of her fate smote her, and she saw instinctively the fierce plunge of those weapons, the long strips of living flesh torn from her bones, the agony, the quivering disgust, itself a worse agony,--while by her side, and holding her in his great lithe embrace, the monster crouched, his white tusks whetting and gnashing, his eyes glaring through all the darkness like balls of red fire,--a shriek, that rang in every forest hollow, that startled every winter-housed thing, that stirred and woke the least needle of the tasselled pines, tore through her lips. A moment afterward, the beast left the arm, once white, now crimson, and looked up alertly.

She did not think at this instant to call upon God. She called upon her husband. It seemed to her that she had but one friend in the world; that was he; and again the cry, loud, clear, prolonged, echoed through the woods. It was not the shriek that disturbed the creature at his relish; he was not born in the woods to be scared of an owl, you know; what then? It must have been the echo, most musical, most resonant, repeated and yet repeated, dying with long sighs of sweet sound, vibrated from rock to river and back again from depth to depth of cave and cliff. Her thought flew after it; she knew, that, even if her husband heard it, he yet could not reach her in time; she saw that while the beast listened he would not gnaw,--and this she *felt* directly, when the rough, sharp, and multiplied stings of his tongue retouched her arm. Again her lips opened by instinct, but the sound that issued thence came by reason. She had heard that music charmed wild beasts,--just this point between life and death intensified every faculty,--and when she opened her lips the third time, it was not for shrieking, but for singing.

A little thread of melody stole out, a rill of tremulous motion; it was the cradle-song with which she rocked her baby;--how could she sing that? And then she remembered the baby sleeping rosily on the long settee before the fire,--the father cleaning his gun, with one foot on the green wooden rundle,--the merry light from the chimney dancing out and through the room, on the rafters of the ceiling with their tassels of onions and herbs, on the log walls painted with lichens and festooned with apples, on the king's-arm slung across the shelf with the old pirate's-cutlass, on the snow-pile of the bed, and on the great brass clock,--dancing, too, and lingering on the baby, with his fringed-gentian eyes, his chubby fists clenched on the pillow, and his fine breezy hair fanning with the motion of his father's foot. All this struck her in one, and made a sob of her breath, and she ceased.

Immediately the long red tongue thrust forth again. Before it touched, a song sprang to her lips, a wild sea-song, such as some sailor might be singing far out on trackless blue water that night, the shrouds whistling with frost and the sheets glued in ice,--a song with the wind in its burden and the spray in its chorus. The monster raised his head and flared the fiery eyeballs upon her, then fretted the imprisoned claws a moment and was quiet; only the breath like the vapor from some hell-pit still swathed her. Her voice, at first faint and fearful, gradually lost its quaver, grew under her control and subject to her modulation; it rose on long swells, it fell in subtile cadences, now and then its tones pealed out like bells from distant belfries on fresh sonorous mornings. She sung the song through, and, wondering lest his name of Indian Devil were not his true name, and if he would not detect her, she repeated it. Once or twice now, indeed, the beast stirred uneasily, turned, and made the bough sway at his movement. As she ended, he snapped his jaws together, and tore away the fettered member, curling it under him with a snarl,--when she burst into the gayest reel that ever answered a fiddle-bow. How many a time she had heard her husband play it on the homely fiddle made by himself from birch and cherry-wood! how many a time she had seen it danced on the floor of their one room, to the patter of wooden clogs and the rustle of homespun petticoat! how many a time she had danced it herself!--and did she not remember once, as they joined clasps for eight-hands-round, how it had lent its gay, bright measure to her life? And here she was singing it alone, in the forest, at midnight, to a wild beast! As she sent her voice trilling up and down its quick oscillations between joy and pain, the creature who grasped her uncurled his paw and scratched the bark from the bough; she must vary the spell; and her voice spun leaping along the projecting points of tune of a hornpipe. Still singing, she felt herself twisted about with a low growl and a lifting of the red lip from the glittering teeth; she broke the hornpipe's thread, and commenced unravelling a lighter, livelier thing, an Irish jig. Up and down and round about her voice flew, the beast threw back his head so that the diabolical face fronted hers, and the torrent of his breath prepared her for his feast as the anaconda slimes his prey. Franticly she darted from tune to tune; his restless movements followed her. She tired herself with dancing and vivid national airs, growing feverish and singing spasmodically as she felt her horrid tomb yawning wider. Touching in this manner all the slogan and keen clan cries, the beast moved again, but only to lay the disengaged paw across her with heavy satisfaction. She did not dare to pause; through the clear cold air, the frosty starlight, she sang. If there were yet any tremor in the tone, it was not fear,--she had learned the secret of sound at last; nor could it be chill,--far too high a fever throbbed her pulses; it was nothing but the thought of the log-house and of what might be passing within it. She fancied the baby stirring in his sleep and moving his pretty lips,--her husband rising and opening the door, looking out after her, and wondering at her absence. She fancied the light pouring through the chink and then shut in again with all the safety and comfort and joy, her husband taking down the fiddle and playing lightly with his head inclined, playing while she sang, while she sang for her life to an Indian Devil. Then she knew he was fumbling for and finding some shining fragment and scoring it down the yellowing hair, and unconsciously her voice forsook the wild war-tunes and drifted into the half-gay, half-melancholy Rosin the Bow.

Suddenly she woke pierced with a pang, and the daggered tooth penetrating her flesh;--dreaming of safety, she had ceased singing and lost it. The beast had regained the use of all his limbs, and now, standing and raising his back, bristling and foaming, with sounds that would have been like hisses but for their deep and fearful sonority, he withdrew step by step toward the trunk of the tree, still with his flaming balls upon her. She was all at once free, on one end of the bough, twenty feet from the ground. She did not measure the distance, but rose to drop herself down, careless of any death, so that it were not this. Instantly, as if he scanned her thoughts, the creature bounded forward with a yell and caught her again in his dreadful hold. It might be that he was not greatly famished; for, as she suddenly flung up her voice again, he settled himself composedly on the bough, still clasping her with invincible pressure to his rough, ravenous breast, and listening in a fascination to the sad, strange U-la-lu that now moaned forth in loud, hollow tones above him. He half closed his eyes, and sleepily reopened and shut them again.

What rending pains were close at hand! Death! and what a death! worse than any other that is to be named! Water, be it cold or warm, that which buoys up blue ice-fields, or which bathes tropical coasts with currents of balmy bliss, is yet a gentle conqueror, kisses as it kills, and draws you down gently through darkening fathoms to its heart. Death at the sword is the festival of trumpet and bugle and banner, with glory ringing out around you and distant hearts thrilling through yours. No gnawing disease can bring such hideous end as this; for that is a fiend bred of your own flesh, and this--is it a fiend, this living lump of appetites? What dread comes with the thought of perishing in flames! but fire, let it leap and hiss never so hotly, is something too remote, too alien, to inspire us with such loathly horror as a wild beast; if it have a life, that life is too utterly beyond our comprehension. Fire is not half ourselves; as it devours, arouses neither hatred nor disgust; is not to be known by the strength of our lower natures let loose; does not drip our blood into our faces from foaming chaps, nor mouth nor slaver above us with vitality. Let us be ended by fire, and we are ashes, for the winds to bear, the leaves to cover; let us be ended by wild beasts, and the base, cursed thing howls with us forever through the forest. All this she felt as she charmed him, and what force it lent to her song God knows. If her voice should fail! If the damp and cold should give her any fatal hoarseness! If all the silent powers of the forest did not conspire to help her! The dark, hollow night rose indifferently over her; the wide, cold air breathed rudely past her, lifted her wet hair and blew it down again; the great boughs swung with a ponderous strength, now and then clashed their iron lengths together and shook off a sparkle of icy spears or some long-lain weight of snow from their heavy shadows. The green depths were utterly cold and silent and stern. These beautiful haunts that all the summer were hers and rejoiced to share with her their bounty, these heavens that had yielded their largess, these stems that had thrust their blossoms into her hands, all these friends of three moons ago forgot her now and knew her no longer.

Feeling her desolation, wild, melancholy, forsaken songs rose thereon from that frightful aerie,--weeping, wailing tunes, that sob among the people from age to age, and overflow with otherwise unexpressed sadness,--all rude, mournful ballads,--old tearful strains, that Shakespeare heard the vagrants sing, and that rise and fall like the wind and tide,--sailor-songs, to be heard only in lone mid-watches beneath the moon and stars,--ghastly rhyming romances, such as that famous one of the Lady Margaret, when

> "She slipped on her gown of green
>   A piece below the knee,--
> And 't was all a long, cold winter's night
>   A dead corse followed she."

Still the beast lay with closed eyes, yet never relaxing his grasp. Once a half-whine of enjoyment escaped him,--he fawned his fearful head upon her; once he scored her cheek with his tongue: savage caresses that hurt like wounds. How weary she was! and yet how terribly awake! How fuller and fuller of dismay grew the knowledge that she was only prolonging her anguish and playing with death! How appalling the thought that with her voice ceased her existence! Yet she could not sing forever; her throat was dry and hard; her very breath was a pain; her mouth was hotter than any desert-worn pilgrim's;--if she could but drop upon her burning tongue one atom of the ice that glittered about her!--but both of her arms were pinioned in the giant's vice. She remembered the winding-sheet, and for the first time in her life shivered with spiritual fear. Was it hers? She asked herself, as she sang, what sins she had committed, what life she had led, to find her punishment so soon and in these pangs,--and then she sought eagerly for some reason why her husband was not up and abroad to find her. He failed her,--her one sole hope in life; and without being aware of it, her voice forsook the songs of suffering and sorrow for old Covenanting hymns,--hymns with which her mother had lulled her, which the class-leader pitched in the chimney-corners,--grand and sweet Methodist hymns, brimming with melody and with all fantastic involutions of tune to suit that ecstatic worship,--hymns full of the beauty of holiness, steadfast, relying, sanctified by the salvation they had lent to those in worse extremity than hers,--for they had found themselves in the grasp of hell, while she was but in the jaws of death. Out of this strange music, peculiar to one character of faith, and than which there is none more beautiful in its degree nor owning a more potent sway of sound, her voice soared into the glorified chants of churches. What to her was death by cold or famine or wild beasts? "Though He slay me, yet will I trust in him," she sang. High and clear through the frore fair night, the level moonbeams splintering in the wood, the scarce glints of stars in the shadowy roof of branches, these sacred anthems rose,-- rose as a hope from despair, as some snowy spray of flower-bells from blackest mould. Was she not in God's hands? Did not the world swing at his will? If this were in his great plan of providence, was it not best, and should she not accept it?

"He is the Lord our God; his judgments are in all the earth."

Oh, sublime faith of our fathers, where utter self-sacrifice alone was true love, the fragrance of whose unrequired subjection was pleasanter than that of golden censers swung in purple-vapored chancels!

Never ceasing in the rhythm of her thoughts, articulated in music as they thronged, the memory of her first communion flashed over her. Again she was in that distant place on that sweet spring morning. Again the congregation rustled out, and the few remained, and she trembled to find herself among them. How well she remembered the devout, quiet faces, too accustomed to the sacred feast to glow with their inner joy! how well the snowy linen at the altar, the silver vessels slowly and silently shifting! and as the cup approached and passed, how the sense of delicious perfume stole in and heightened the transport of her prayer, and she had seemed, looking up through the windows where the sky soared blue in constant freshness, to feel all heaven's balms dripping from the portals, and to scent the lilies of eternal peace! Perhaps another would not have felt so much ecstasy as satisfaction on that occasion; but it is a true, if a later disciple, who has said, "The Lord bestoweth his blessings there, where he findeth the vessels empty."

"And does it need the walls of a church to renew my communion?" she asked. "Does not every moment stand a temple four-square to God? And in that morning, with its buoyant sunlight, was I any dearer to the Heart of the World than now?-- 'My beloved is mine, and I am his," she sang over and over again, with all varied inflection and profuse tune. How gently all the winter-wrapt things bent toward her then! into what relation with her had they grown! how this common dependence was the spell of their intimacy! how at one with Nature had she become! how all the night and the silence and the forest seemed to hold its breath, and to send its soul up to God in her singing! It was no longer despondency, that singing. It was neither prayer nor petition. She had left imploring, "How long wilt thou forget me, O Lord? Lighten mine eyes, lest I sleep the sleep of death! For in death there is no remembrance of thee,"--with countless other such fragments of supplication. She cried rather, "Yea, though I walk through the valley of the shadow of death, I will fear no evil: for thou art with me; thy rod and thy staff, they comfort me,"--and lingered, and repeated, and sang again, "I shall be satisfied, when I awake, with thy likeness."

Then she thought of the Great Deliverance, when he drew her up out of many waters, and the flashing old psalm pealed forth triumphantly:--

"The lord descended from above,
    and bow'd the heavens hie:
And underneath his feet he cast
    the darknesse of the skie.
On cherubs and on cherubins
    full royally he road:
And on the wings of all the winds
    came flying all abroad."

She forgot how recently, and with what a strange pity for her own shapeless form that was to be, she had quaintly sung,--

"Oh, lovely appearance of death!
    What sight upon earth is so fair?
Not all the gay pageants that breathe
    Can with a dead body compare!"

She remembered instead,--"In thy presence is fulness of joy; at thy right hand there are pleasures forevermore. God will redeem my soul from the power of the grave: for he shall receive me. He will swallow up death in victory." Not once now did she say, "Lord, how long wilt thou look on? rescue my soul from their destructions, my darling from the lions,"--for she knew that the young lions roar after their prey and seek their meat from God. "O Lord, thou preservest man and beast!" she said.

She had no comfort or consolation in this season, such as sustained the Christian martyrs in the amphitheatre. She was not dying for her faith; there were no palms in heaven for her to wave; but how many a time had she declared,--"I had rather be a doorkeeper in the house of my God, than to dwell in the tents of wickedness!" And as the broad rays here and there broke through the dense covert of shade and lay in rivers of lustre on crystal sheathing and frozen fretting of trunk and limb and on the great spaces of refraction, they builded up visibly that house, the shining city on the hill, and singing, "Beautiful for situation, the joy of the whole earth, is Mount Zion, on the sides of the North, the city of the Great King," her vision climbed to that higher picture where the angel shows the dazzling thing, the holy Jerusalem descending out of heaven from God, with its splendid battlements and gates of pearls, and its foundations, the eleventh a jacinth, the twelfth an amethyst,--with its great white throne, and the rainbow round about it, in sight like unto an emerald: "And there shall be no night there,--for the Lord God giveth them light," she sang.

What whisper of dawn now rustled through the wilderness? How the night was passing! And still the beast crouched upon the bough, changing only the posture of his head, that again he might command her with those charmed eyes;--half their fire was gone; she could almost have released herself from his custody; yet, had she stirred, no one knows what malevolent instinct might have dominated anew. But of that she did not dream; long ago stripped of any expectation, she was experiencing in her divine rapture how mystically true it is that "he that dwelleth in the secret place of the Most High shall abide under the shadow of the Almighty."

Slow clarion cries now wound from the distance as the cocks caught the intelligence of day and re-echoed it faintly from farm to farm,--sleepy sentinels of night, sounding the foe's invasion, and translating that dim intuition to ringing notes of warning. Still she chanted on. A remote crash of brushwood told of some other beast on his depredations, or some night-belated traveller groping his way through the narrow path. Still she chanted on. The far, faint echoes of the chanticleers died into distance,--the crashing of the branches grew nearer. No wild beast that, but a man's step,--a man's form in the moonlight, stalwart and strong,--on one arm slept a little child, in the other hand he held his gun. Still she chanted on.

Perhaps, when her husband last looked forth, he was half ashamed to find what a fear he felt for her. He knew she would never leave the child so long but for some direst need,--and yet he may have laughed at himself, as he lifted and wrapped it with awkward care, and, loading his gun and strapping on his horn, opened the door again and closed it behind him, going out and plunging into the darkness and dangers of the forest. He was more singularly alarmed than he would have been willing to acknowledge; as he had sat with his bow hovering over the strings, he had half believed to hear her voice mingling gayly with the instrument, till he paused and listened if she were not about to lift the latch and enter. As he drew nearer the heart of the forest, that intimation of melody seemed to grow more actual, to take body and breath, to come and go on long swells and ebbs of the night-breeze, to increase with tune and words, till a strange shrill singing grew ever clearer, and, as he stepped into an open space of moonbeams, far up in the branches, rocked by the wind, and singing, "How beautiful upon the mountains are the feet of him that bringeth good tidings, that publisheth peace," he saw his wife,--his wife,--but, great God in heaven! how? Some mad exclamation escaped him, but without diverting her. The child knew the singing voice, though never heard before in that unearthly key, and turned toward it through the veiling dreams. With a celerity almost instantaneous, it lay, in the twinkling of an eye, on the ground at the father's feet, while his gun was raised to his shoulder and levelled at the monster covering his wife with shaggy form and flaming gaze,--his wife so ghastly white, so rigid, so stained with blood, her eyes so fixedly bent above, and her lips, that had indurated into the chiselled pallor of marble, parted only with that flood of solemn song.

I do not know if it were the mother-instinct that for a moment lowered her eyes,--those eyes, so lately riveted on heaven, now suddenly seeing all life-long bliss possible. A thrill of joy pierced and shivered through her like a weapon, her voice trembled in its course, her glance lost its steady strength, fever-flushes chased each other over her face, yet she never once ceased chanting. She was quite aware, that, if her husband shot now, the ball must pierce her body before reaching any vital part of the beast,--and yet better that death, by his hand, than the other. But this her husband also knew, and he remained motionless, just covering the creature with the sight. He dared not fire, lest some wound not mortal should break the spell exercised by her voice, and the beast, enraged with pain, should rend her in atoms; moreover, the light was too uncertain for his aim. So he waited. Now and then he examined his gun to see if the damp were injuring its charge, now and then he wiped the great drops from his forehead. Again the cocks crowed with the passing hour,--the last time they were heard on that night. Cheerful home sound then, how full of safety and all comfort and rest it seemed! what sweet morning incidents of sparkling fire and sunshine, of gay household bustle, shining dresser, and cooing baby, of steaming cattle in the yard, and brimming milk-pails at the door! what pleasant voices! what laughter! what security! and here--

Now, as she sang on in the slow, endless, infinite moments, the fervent vision of God's peace was gone. Just as the grave had lost its sting, she was snatched back again into the arms of earthly hope. In vain she tried to sing, "There remaineth a rest for the people of God,"-- her eyes trembled on her husband's, and she could only think of him, and of the child, and of happiness that yet might be, but with what a dreadful gulf of doubt between! She shuddered now in the suspense; all calm forsook her; she was tortured with dissolving heats or frozen with icy blasts; her face contracted, growing small and pinched; her voice was hoarse and sharp,--every tone cut like a knife,--the notes became heavy to lift,-- withheld by some hostile pressure,--impossible. One gasp, a convulsive effort, and there was silence,--she had lost her voice.

The beast made a sluggish movement,--stretched and fawned like one awakening,--then, as if he would have yet more of the enchantment, stirred her slightly with his muzzle. As he did so, a sidelong hint of the man standing below with the raised gun smote him; he sprung round furiously, and, seizing his prey, was about to leap into some unknown airy den of the topmost branches now waving to the slow dawn. The late moon had rounded through the sky so that her gleam at last fell full upon the bough with fairy frosting; the wintry morning light did not yet penetrate the gloom. The woman, suspended in mid-air an instant, cast only one agonized glance beneath,--but across and through it, ere the lids could fall, shot a withering sheet of flame,--a rifle-crack, half-heard, was lost in the terrible yell of desperation that bounded after it and filled her ears with savage echoes, and in the wide arc of some eternal descent she was falling;--but the beast fell under her.

I think that the moment following must have been too sacred for us, and perhaps the three have no special interest again till they issue from the shadows of the wilderness upon the white hills that skirt their home. The father carries the child hushed again into slumber, the mother follows with no such feeble step as might be anticipated. It is not time for reaction,--the tension not yet relaxed, the nerves still vibrant, she seems to herself like some one newly made; the night was a dream; the present stamped upon her in deep satisfaction, neither weighed nor compared with the past; if she has the careful tricks of former habit, it is as an automaton; and as they slowly climb the steep under the clear gray vault and the paling morning star, and as she stops to gather a spray of the red-rose berries or a feathery tuft of dead grasses for the chimney-piece of the log-house, or a handful of brown cones for the child's play,--of these quiet, happy folk you would scarcely dream how lately they had stolen from under the banner and encampment of the great King Death. The husband proceeds a step or two in advance; the wife lingers over a singular foot-print in the snow, stoops and examines it, then looks up with a hurried word. Her husband stands alone on the hill, his arms folded across the babe, his gun fallen,--stands defined as a silhouette against the pallid sky. What is there in their home, lying below and yellowing in the light, to fix him with such a stare? She springs to his side. There is no home there. The log-house, the barns, the neighboring farms, the fences, are all blotted out and mingled in one smoking ruin. Desolation and death were indeed there, and beneficence and life in the forest. Tomahawk and scalping-knife, descending during that night, had left behind them only this work of their accomplished hatred and one subtle foot-print in the snow.

For the rest,--the world was all before them, where to choose.